The March Effect

by

Kim Alexander

The March Effect

Editor: Carly Hayward of Book Light Editorial

Cover Art: Pretty AF Designs

Formatted for Print: Pretty AF Designs

Praise for Pure:

New World Magic Book One

"I love this story! It rivals the best urban fantasy books that I have ever read."— Diana, Audible Reviewer

"Kim embraces the writing style of Ilona Andrews and Jeaniene Frost with snarky heroines, exciting plotlines, and of course mythical creatures"— Nerd Girl Official

"Captivating Read! Fantasy/Romance/Mystery writers, move over in a big way for the new kid on the dark street who can write plot and dialogue as clever and quick as Nora Roberts"

— Rad Dad, Amazon Reviewer

Praise for Kim Alexander

"Kim Alexander's *The Sand Prince* is a thrill ride of fantastical proportion. Can hardly wait for the next wild installment."
— David Baldacci, New York Times and International Best-Selling Author

"The Sand Prince is a wonder — full of magic, drama and sly humor. Kim Alexander might just be a wizard."
— Daniel Stashower, New York Times Best-selling Author

"I love these characters (even the horrible ones) and their growth and depth; I love the world(s)-building and the not-quite-hereness of it and the utterly beautiful and unique story." — Tracet, NetGalley Reviewer

"FIVE STARS! Unique characters and interesting writing."
— Mark, Amazon Reviewer

THE MARCH EFFECT

KIM ALEXANDER

9·18·21

1

The coffee cup floated right past me.

"What the what?" I yelped, pushing myself away from the hovering mug. I bounced off the chair and landed on my butt on the floor.

Everyone in the coffee shop turned to stare.

"I'm fine," I announced, though no one had asked. I carefully plucked the cup from where it hovered a foot or so above the table and replaced it on the scratched Formica. After a few seconds, I let go. It stayed put. It happened so quickly I didn't think anyone got their phones out, so I'd be spared being the 'weird-girl-in-diner' on Instagram. A couple of kids did seem to be paying attention, but they don't use Instagram, do they?

I'd already been media famous once, almost nine years ago. That time, first I was 'Victim A,' then I was 'Coral Gables woman injured in vampire attack,' and finally 'College student recovering after near-deadly xeno encounter struggles to pick up the pieces of her life.'

I still had the scrapbook of cuttings from the newspapers, and since March had healed the ugly scars on my throat, those yellowing clips were all I had left. Well, that and a new perspective on xenos. I now understood they weren't all slavering, stinking monsters. After all, Dr. Bel, the therapist who turned things around for me, turned out to not only be a demi-goddess, but also the ex-girlfriend of March.

March, the unicorn. And sometimes, human man.

I saved his life. He saved mine. Then he vanished.

My life went back to normal after he left me, but normal wasn't necessarily better. Of course, I missed him. He was beautiful, kind, brave, great in bed (great doesn't really do the job, TBH) and yeah, an actual unicorn. But I was careful not to make more of it than it was—I never said 'love' out loud. I barely whispered it to myself. I knew how he was. When he desired something, it came to him. He didn't even do it on purpose. In my head (I never even told Dr. Bel this), I started calling it the March Effect. Did he want me to love him? Or was it just that he expected to be admired and adored, and my brain read that as 'fall in love?' I'd probably never know, since he made it pretty clear when he healed my scars that he was done with the human world. Not that I blame him for leaving—from Margaret trying to saw his horn off to losing his magical abilities for a week, to Baba Yaga almost cutting out his heart, I'm sure he had a lot to process. I know I did.

I waited for the cup to do something else, but it just steamed and sat there. I took a tentative sip. Just coffee. Maybe I'd hallucinated the moving mug, just like over the last few weeks I'd dreamed up the single soup can sitting in the bathtub, the TV remote in the freezer, the slowly rotating tower of books floating an inch above my bed. As if to remind me of the forces at play just out of sight, the cup gave a jerking twitch between my hands, like a hamster trying to escape, and then it was still. I shut off my laptop and got out of there. The coffee was getting cold, and anyway, it was time to head to work at the bar voted #53rd Friendliest in D.C. five years in a row, where the ice is warm, and you only get one bar on your phone, the bar that put the 'die' in dive: The Hare.

2

Work that night was normal, with the exception of Claudio acting like he was in the third act of a horror movie, all wide worried eyes and looking over his shoulder.

"What's up?" I asked at his fifth dramatic sigh.

He refilled my ice bin, then froze, holding the bucket in midair. "No. Nothing. Never mind."

Is there anything more annoying than someone who obviously wants you to make a big deal out of asking them what's wrong? As The Hare began to empty out, the music faded from Curtis Mayfield to the spa mix we use to chill ourselves down. I was looking forward to the small pleasures that waited for me at home: taking off my bra, opening a beer, sitting on the couch with leftovers and House Hunters. Tonight it would be pizza and Reykjavik. Truly, it's a non-stop thrill ride at my place.

"Okay, for real. What is wrong with you?" Claudio gave me big innocent eyes, but I wasn't having it. He fiddled with the charms woven into his long braids, as he always did when he was nervous. He went right for the icon of St. Kentigern, the one you invoke when you're being bullied. "Let go of that thing, he won't help you now. You've been acting hinky all night. What's going on?"

He leaned against the cooler, flinging the assortment of tokens over his shoulder. "I wasn't going to tell you, but fine. I saw Marly."

My heart contracted painfully, and I tried not let it show. All I wanted to do for these last few months was talk to Marly, but she made it clear the last time I saw her she was done talking to me. "So?"

"So? Really?" My 'I don't care' act was no better than his 'nothing to report' act. We knew each other too well. "It was last month. The first time."

"First time?" I got ready to holler at him, but he cut me off.

"The first time she was in the CVS by me. She didn't have much to say. In fact, she acted like she didn't see me. But I followed her around, and she finally said she was fine and busy and she had to go. She dropped her basket and took off. I knew you two had just... talked about what happened, and I kind of blew it off at the time." He looked uncomfortable. 'Talked about what happened' was a nice way of describing it. It took months for me to tell Marly the truth, long after it happened, after March brought her back from wherever she was while a vampire was using her body. I went back and forth—I didn't want to tell her at all, and then I knew that was stupid and dishonest, and she deserved better. She deserved to know. I had to tell her. I couldn't tell her. Christmas and Solstice and New Year came and went, and I acted like her friend, even though it was all a lie. 'Talked about what happened.' Yeah, there was some talking. But there was also some yelling and some crying. And then, nothing.

"What are you not telling me?" I asked.

"Well, she was wearing sunglasses."

"In the store? I guess that's kind of strange."

"In the store at 3 a.m. And she had a big bandage taped to the inside of her elbow. Like from a blood test." He sighed again. "But the second time, she was still wearing the sunglasses in the middle of the night, and it was out on Columbia Road. And she looked kind of... like ass? Like she hadn't taken a shower in a while? And she said not to tell you I saw her. Sorry."

"Thanks for telling me. I'm sorry you got sucked in. I'm sure she's okay." I wasn't sure at all. I paused to pour a beer and make some change. Then I turned back to him. "What was in her basket?"

"I...um, God, it was a while ago. Let me think.

Alcohol. A bottle of rubbing alcohol. Band-Aids. And gauze. Oh, and oven mitts. Is that weird?"

"I don't know," I said. "Maybe she started a meth lab?" The bandage made it sound like she'd gone to a doctor. That was good, right? It had to be. If she was... still not back to being herself, to being fully human, she wouldn't have risked someone finding out. And she wouldn't be wandering around the drug store, she'd be out. Hunting

Anyway, how could I know why she was wearing night time sunglasses? Maybe she had an allergic reaction to some expired mascara or something.

No, that was stupid. I couldn't rationalize or explain it away. Something wasn't right, and I had to find out what it was.

Like it sometimes did, things picked up right before closing, so we didn't get to talk further. I served drinks, and Claudio washed glasses and ran kegs. Finally, the pace slowed, and I took a minute to stretch my back. I closed my eyes and rolled my head from side-to-side. When I opened them, I was face to face with a girl who'd practically launched herself across the bar at me.

"HI! HI YOU'RE HER! HI, RUBY!" The young woman didn't need to yell, the music wasn't that loud, but she was grinning at me like I was the cutest puppy on the internet. Then I guess she saw the look on my face and started laughing. "Sorry. I'm just super excited to finally meet you!"

Some people knew who I was from what happened in Florida, but they were usually way older. It had been ages since I ran into one of them. I took a deep breath and launched into my prepared speech.

"I really don't have anything to say about—"

"Oh, come on! Sure you do!" Then she shook her head. "I'm such a dope! Hi, I'm Lauren C, and I'll be your investigator!" She stuck out her hand. Her nails were sparkly green, and so were her eyes. I took a closer look.

"Hi, Lauren C," I said slowly. Then I took her hand, because it seemed rude to leave a xeno hanging. "What kind of investigator?"

"From the Seelie Court, of course." She gave me a brisk handshake. "You had a busy year, and the court decided to launch an inquiry." Her eyes got even bigger. "Unicorns and vampires, and who knows what else! The court is very interested." The fae kept to themselves and decidedly did not try and assimilate with the mortal population. I'd never seen one before, and I didn't know much about the fae court, other than words like 'heartless' and 'debauched' came up a lot. Lauren didn't look like either one; more like the edgiest cheerleader on the squad.

"You got sent here by the actual Fairy Queen? That is badass." Claudio set a bowl of wasabi peas in front of Lauren. "Love your hair."

The fae brushed her hand through her dark pixie

cut, the kind I always admired from afar. If I cut my hair that short, I'd look like a volleyball. "Thanks. Are you Claudio? You are, right?" He said he was, and she bounced in her seat a little. "This is going even better than I hoped it would! Oh, and there's no fairy 'queen,' not like you mean it. We've moved to a parliamentary system. We had a constitutional monarchy until the last queen retired about seven hundred years ago. I think she lives in Florida now. Not like those freaks in the Unseelie. They loooove their king." She gave a delicate shudder, then glanced curiously at my head. "What's up with that?"

"Whoa, are you doing that?" Claudio gaped at me. I looked up to see a salt shaker, two limes and a trio of shot glasses orbiting about a foot above my head. I reached up and yanked everything down, setting it on the bar. He looked at me gravely. "This can only mean one thing." I waited. He held up his hand. "Magic wants us to do shots!"

"Yay shots!" Lauren chimed in. "I know what those are!" She laughed and started writing with her fingertip onto her other palm. I could see faint traces of light in her hand. "But seriously." She looked up at me. "What was that?"

I sighed. Maybe I shouldn't have spilled my guts to a xeno interrogator, but it was possible she'd know what was going on, and after all, I wasn't doing anything anti-Seelie as far as I knew. I decided to risk it. "I don't know.

It's been happening for the last few weeks. Things moving on their own, the shower turns itself on, my dishes rearrange themselves...but I don't know why. I don't think I'm doing it."

Lauren nodded enthusiastically. "Thoughts. I have thoughts," she told me. "This is exactly the sort of thing I came here for. We'll talk about it." Claudio handed me a shot of tequila. I set up the salt and lime and downed it. Lauren did her shot, and we spent the next five minutes pounding her on the back and helpfully telling her to put her hands up. Claudio handed her a bar nap, and she wiped her streaming eyes. Once she could breathe again, she sighed mournfully and said, "Shots look more fun on TV."

"You guys watch a lot of TV at the, uh, court?" I asked.

"Of course. I watched seven seasons of *The Bachelor* and five of *The Bachelorette* to prepare to come here. Not *Bachelors in Paradise*, though. That's trash."

"Oh, come on," said Claudio. "That's the only good one." We both gave him a hard look. "Well, it is!"

"That's where I picked my mortal name," she continued. "From my studies, it's clear that Lauren is the most desirable name for human females. The C," she concluded, "stands for Seelie."

"Sounds legit," I agreed. "What's your real name?"

She opened her mouth, and music came out. Like bells, or wind chimes, but purple and pink along with the sound.

"Okay," I said. "Lauren it is. So, am I making a mistake by talking to you? Am I in trouble? Do I need a lawyer?"

She frowned. "No? I mean, I'm supposed to find out about the unicorn, and why it became so attached to you. He became, I mean." She downed a palmful of peas. "My court is considering an outreach program to the mortal world, and this seemed like a good place to start. You are a sort of intersection, Ruby. A lot of activity around you."

"Hooray for me." She wasn't wrong, though. From those trash vamps in Florida to March, I was putting together quite a xeno resume. But I looped back to her earlier comment. "He was attached to me? He said he was attached to me?" My stupid heart swelled like a balloon. I hadn't realized it had shrunk. "Did you...he told you that?"

"In person? Oh, no. But we hear things."

Sure. I guess from the outside it looked like more than it was. More than it was to him.

Lauren gave me a curious look, but let my deflation go without comment. Then she added, "And what happened with Marly, of course. Will she be here soon?"

Claudio and I exchanged glances, and I thought again about her night time sunglasses. "No," I said. "I don't think she'll be around."

3

Yeah, Marly wasn't likely to show up, except maybe with a weapon. I wasn't her favorite person anymore, and I can't say I blame her.

Speaking of passing around some blame, the last time I saw Dr. Bel, the weather was warming up, the cherry trees were just about over, and I couldn't stand to look at myself in the mirror.

"I can't tell you what to do, Ruby." Dr. Bel was almost as tired of my hesitation as I was. "You know what to do."

"But I'm afraid if I tell her, I'll lose her." I could picture the way it would happen. Tears. Rage. Hair-pulling. Broken bottles. Does rage re-induce vampirism? I might get to find out. And I would deserve it. How could she forgive me?

"If you are going to lose her, if that's the decision

she makes, it has already happened. Waiting won't change that, it'll only make it worse." She fiddled with her pen. I bet she wanted to stab me with it. "You may be underestimating your friend. She may not blame you at all. Remember, you didn't turn her."

"But it happened because of me." I reached for another tissue. It was so unfair. My life had turned out just fine. I was probably a more emotionally together person now than I was before I ran into that blonde bitch Margaret on the street in the middle of the night. I made that split-second decision (which was no decision) to save March from her gang of poachers, and I got a gorgeous, magical lover. Sure it was scary and awful at the time, but I got to be brave, and I got to see real power at work. Poor Marly, who was only trying to protect me, her reward was to get turned into the nastiest, dirtiest thing in the world—even in this new world. The thought of Margaret's smug smile after she turned her made me tear up from anger and frustration, which in turn only made me feel weaker. "She should have just given them my damned keys."

"That was also her decision." She sighed. "I know we've talked about how this has to come from you, but I feel like at this point, I would be failing both of you if I didn't say that you have an obligation to tell her. Not only because it's the right thing to do, but in case there are any future...health concerns."

I looked up, forgetting to cry over my sorry self.

"Will there be?"

She shrugged. "As far as I know, this is the first time someone has been brought back. Not from the dead. That's happened. Back from being a vampire. If it was me, I'd want a blood test." She folded her arms and sat back. *Your move, Ruby.*

My stomach churned. Marly had been so dirty, her new little fangs had torn up the inside of her mouth. I couldn't stop picturing her hands—her nails had been caked with filth. "Oh my God, I didn't even think of that. You think she's infected with something?"

"It would be unethical and unwise for me to speculate. All I'm saying is if Marly was my daughter—or my dear friend—I would suggest blood work." She tore a sheet from her prescription pad and scribbled a name and number. "He's an acquaintance of mine. I'll tell him to be expecting her call."

After that conversation, I knew I didn't have a choice. It was another two days before I saw Marly again, now cut loose from the guy she'd been seeing (he got back together with his kid's mom) and back on her favorite bar stool.

Finally, after everyone left The Hare to the dolorous voice of Gordon Lightfoot and his merry band of dead sailors, I poured her a bourbon and told her to sit back down. I looked past her at the new leaves on the gingko trees outside the window, turned pastel orange in the light of the streetlamps. I knew things would look different after tonight.

“What? You don’t want me to sweep?” She plopped herself back down. “You look funny. What’s up?” Her eyes widened. “Is March back? Have you heard from him?” I didn’t like to talk about him, but she knew. She could tell by the way I yanked my head up every time the door opened and someone that wasn’t him walked in.

“No,” I told her, “but it’s sort of about him. It’s mostly about you.” I grabbed a damp rag and began wiping the bar.

She frowned. “What about me?”

I took a deep breath and dove in. “Remember when he woke you up, when you blacked out?”

She nodded slowly. “I woke up with a bitch of a hangover on the hood of your car. Good times.”

“You weren’t drunk.”

“Oh yeah?” She sipped her drink. “Then I was right, I got roofied. By that Margaret chick.”

“Margaret. Yeah, she had a hand in it. But no, you weren’t drugged.” She raised a brow and looked at me expectantly. “Margaret...she wanted to hurt me. Or show me what she could do... something. She. She had you turned. You were turned.”

“Turned? Turned into what?” Then she realized. There was only one thing people called ‘turned.’ “Whaaaa...” Her voice trailed off and she stared, shocked. “I’m a—”

"No," I said. "No, you aren't. You're not. But for two days, you were."

Her hand flew to cover her mouth. "Oh my God. Did I kill anyone? And you—you saw me?"

"It was before I went to Chicago. Right after it happened, after you got turned. You were...it wasn't you." I'd never tell her what she'd said to me, how she looked utterly insane. Or how she smelled. But the way she was looking at me right then, the disgust, the anger—I deserved it.

"That's...over six months. You knew all this time? Why didn't you tell me before? And did I? Kill anyone? And how...how did I turn back?"

I was too embarrassed to tell her it hadn't even occurred to me, that she might have killed someone. "I don't think you hurt anyone. I don't know. I was in Chicago the whole time."

She hopped off the barstool and began to pace. "You don't know. I could have killed someone. If anyone finds out, I'll get fired. I'll go to jail. And what if there's still some weird shit in my blood?" She looked at her hands, she was starting to panic. "And you've just been keeping this to yourself?"

"I...should have told you sooner. But I didn't know how." I didn't think she was really listening to me.

"Who? Who exactly did this to me?" I opened my mouth, but nothing happened. "Tell me!"

"It was the vamp girl who was working for Margaret.

They wanted to get in to my house, and you wouldn't give them the keys. So..."

"So? So the solution wasn't to break a window? They fucking killed me?" She touched her throat, feeling for marks. I knew there weren't any. "Oh my God. I feel sick."

"It wasn't you," I said. And it really wasn't. Most people believed that when a person got turned, it was the same as being dead. Something from outside made the corpse get up and move around. Vamps weren't reliable narrators, so no one knew for sure. "Whatever happened, it wasn't your fault. I—this is my fault."

"You're damned right it's your fault. Jesus, Ruby—and I guess you're also telling me that March brought me back?"

"Yes." I wiped the bar with the rag, the same spot, over and over. "He brought you back. He gave you back your life. There's nothing bad in your blood. He brought you back, and you're perfect."

She laughed. It sounded like she wanted to scream. "Should I send him flowers?" She wiped her face, she was crying now. "I have to go. I have to...I don't know. Find out if I hurt anyone. God, how could you not tell me?" She held her hand up, and I noticed she had an angry, fresh burn on her palm. "Don't say you're sorry."

"What happened to your hand?"

"Fuck my hand. This isn't like you dented my car. And I know it was a whole *thing*, what happened to you.

And it sucked. You got hurt. He's gone. But I listened to you cry and fed you and...you slept on my couch, and you knew this, the whole time? That I was disgusting, dead thing?" She looked like she wanted to throw up. "Give me my bag." Her purse was stashed behind the bar, and before she snatched it out of my hands, I shoved the paper Dr. Bel gave me inside. She rooted around and pulled out her keys, heading for the stairs.

"Mar, you shouldn't drive, you're too upset." Even while I was saying it, I knew it sounded stupid.

She said "Fuck you," over her shoulder, and slammed the door on her way out.

Claudio says she'll come around in time, but I don't think he really believes that. I do. I have to make this right. I just wish I knew how.

4

So, I was short Marly, but up a new friend/ shadow in Lauren C. After giving her a thorough grilling, Shanti agreed it was safe for me to answer her questions.

Its funny how I went from being a total xenophobe to having so many in my life. March, of course. And Dr. Bel, although I didn't know what she was for most of our relationship. To be honest, I'm still not entirely sure where a demi-goddess falls on the xeno spectrum, only that she's important and respected. Then there's Shanti, Dr. Bel's office manager—at least, that's what the sign on her desk says. But she's much more than that. She's a harpy, a hunter. I've seen her in that body—an eagle-woman the size of a horse, with brilliant orange eyes and a face like a Roman statue. She's also addicted to Korean beauty products and loves margaritas. She's become a regular at The Hare and in my life.

"She seems to be what she says she is." Shanti frowned. "Either that or the fae are way better liars than I've heard." The fae, she explained, weren't supposed to lie at all. They could twist the truth like a balloon animal, but breaking it outright seemed to be against Seelie ethics. "She's here to find out what happened last year and report back to her court. Not sure if she's more interested in Marly or March, but if you're willing to talk to her, she's going to ask about them. So, be prepared. Anyway, I'm taking her to get her settled in her new place. Want to come?"

If you live in D.C., chances are you've passed abandoned buildings. Big ones, old ones. You've probably seen them while you walk your dog, or on your way home from the Metro. They're boarded up and have those neon 'No Trespassing' signs pasted to the windows. Maybe you've wanted to take a look inside, wipe off the soot and peek through a cracked pane. But you didn't. You got distracted, and you walked away. They're all over town, places like that, and with property values being sky high, maybe you've wondered how it was possible for something so large, so obviously valuable, to be simply gathering dust.

Xeno housing is how. There's plenty of them who prefer accommodations beyond alleys, culverts, or deep forests, and just like humans, they need places to live. And even though there are limitless kinds of xenos and they don't all get along, they prefer to stay among themselves. They also really like privacy. They might be traveling on business or here visiting, maybe taking in the sites, going to the museums. Some found the apartments good enough to live in permanently, although Shanti said she was glad to trade it in when she found her rental in Shaw. She and Lauren C. were going to pick up the keys to a place on ___ Street. (Sorry, the glamour extends to even saying the address out loud, and obviously, writing it down is straight out.)

Shanti led the two of us down a trash-strewn alley, to a graffiti'd wall. I found that I strongly wanted to go back the way we came. "So far," I told them, "I love it. Perfect place to dump a body. Shan, you're sure about this?"

They laughed at me, not unkindly. Shanti blew on her palm and placed it against thc brick, and I understood why they found my confusion so funny. The feeling of unease vanished. The alley, now free of any sort of litter, was red brick in a charming herringbone pattern, lined with chestnut trees blooming in frothy pink and white. The ugly brick wall melted away to reveal a small apartment building with an elegant Victorian facade, complete with a turret and a deep front porch. The doorman (well, door troll) let us in, and the building manager, an Asian woman in her thirties named Tha, came out from her office to greet us. I'll be damned if I could figure out what variety of xeno she was, but of course asking "What are you?" is just as rude as asking a fellow human "Where are you from?" when you mean "Where were your parents born?"

Tha remembered Shanti from her stay several years before and greeted Lauren C. like an honored guest. I guess they don't get many fae passing through. Then she looked at me.

"Miss Shanti, you keep interesting company." I think by 'interesting' she meant 'You'd better have a good reason for bringing a mortal in my house.'

"This is my friend Ruby. She's the one with the unicorn."

I died a little. Is that how everyone knew me? I guess unicorn girl is better than vampire bite girl. At any rate, Tha gave me a chilly nod and gave Lauren the key. It was an old-fashioned brass key, not a plastic pass card like hotels now use. "You'll like it here," she said to Lauren. "And your timing is good; a one bedroom just opened up. A selkie lived there. Nice girl, but she had to go back home to the Orkneys in a hurry. So, twenty-four hour coffee and water on primrose. The gym is in the basement, and we send your laundry out. Your floor is guaranteed iron free." I'd heard that some xenos were allergic to iron, so that made sense, and I figured I'd find out what primrose was sooner or later.

We got on the elevator, and I looked at the floors. They were labeled *dogwood, thistle, primrose, toad,* and *feather* was the penthouse, so there you go. Lauren's place was on *thistle*. We passed a tall woman in a floor length, raggedy black veil in the hallway. Her deteriorating outfit made a sharp contrast to the plush red and cream carpet and the glossy wood paneling. Through the lace I could hear her sobbing. I didn't want to stare, but it looked like her neck was three feet long. She stopped crying long enough to say hello to Tha.

"On your way to work, dear?" The veiled woman nodded. "Give Dr. Bowman my regards. I have to bring the boys in."

She said she'd check the appointment book, then began wailing again. The elevator doors closed and the sound trailed away.

"She's a dental hygienist. Best in town." Tha led us down the hallway, and we came to a stop in front of the right door. We all looked at each other.

"Do you smell something?" Lauren asked. Naturally I mentally ran down my morning hygiene routine, but she didn't mean me.

"Someone better clean their cat box," Shanti observed. Then she got an odd look on her face. She sniffed once, twice, and then shook her head. "Never mind."

"Something weird?" I asked.

"I thought I hit on something bad. With bad intentions, I mean. but there are so many xenos in this building, it would be kind of amazing if someone wasn't in a foul mood." Shanti, as a hunter, could pick a xeno out in a crowd. “Sorry,” she said to Tha. I guess it was kind of intrusive to smell all her tenants.

Tha frowned. “I’ll talk to your neighbor,” she said to Lauren. She gave me another suspicious stare and left.

Lauren’s new home had a galley kitchen and dollhouse-sized bedroom and bathroom. It looked like any mid-priced extended-stay hotel in the country. I guess we were all expecting a flower-strewn bower or something. Lauren tried to hide her disappointment.

“Well,” she said, “At least its open concept!”

“We’ll go shopping, get you some pillows and candles and whatnot,” I said.

“And pedicures,” added Shanti. “To improve our vibes. First one’s on me.”

And that was the beginning of how Lauren C settled into our lives. She and I began a routine of spending an hour or so over lunch nearly every day. She was curious about what we started calling my ‘random magic,’ and she obviously wanted to hear all about March but understood the pain had hardly healed, so she didn’t push. She gave me room to talk about what happened, and I learned about the fae and what her life was like. And as we promised, Shanti and I helped her spruce her little apartment up. She had an unshakeable affinity for fluffy pink crap, and it was kind of endearing to watch the thrill she got from a pompom covered bathmat.

She couldn't believe something just for under your feet could be so pretty.

One afternoon, we were talking about how March and I got involved. She took a lot of notes on her hand.

"I knew I shouldn't have, um, gotten intimate with March that quickly. We had just met, and he was kinda drunk."

She frowned and lifted her fingertip from her palm. "Which part of that is against your kind's principles? Because in my studies what you describe seems to be a required element."

Most of her studies involved reality television. "You know it's not really real, right?"

"But it's *reality* shows." She looked pretty indignant. "It's right there in the name."

"Yeah, but I've heard they're mostly actors. They're acting like they're fighting, or drunk, or in love. Except sometimes the acting spills into real life. It's not exactly real, but it's not completely fake, either."

I couldn't convince her most of our normal human lives weren't so overwrought and dramatic.

We hit another roadblock when I talked about how I grew up in Florida and that my parents now lived in upstate New York. Because of my job and their own travels, I rarely got to see them. When she realized the size of the country and the number of people living here, she was stunned.

"There are only enough of us fae to fill one of your

cities, I think. I don't know about the Unseelie Court, but surely they are not great in numbers either. They say no Unseelie child has been brought into the world since the moon was young." I don't know if she actually believed how many humans live on this planet, or if she was just humoring me, like with the reality of reality TV.

I could talk to Lauren about what happened without being challenged to 'go deeper' or figure out 'why do you feel that way?' And for a fae, a race that got a pretty bad rap, Lauren was good company. She was deeply curious about mortal life and interactions. She was also proud of her position as an investigator, and I think rightly so, even if she was woefully underpaid—or undergifted, I guess. She tried (more than once) to explain how the fae economy worked. It seemed to be based on giving gifts—not to be a pal, but to incur debt.

"This," she said to me, carefully setting a sliver of what looked like a seashell on the bar. "This is my gift."

"A seashell?"

"The shell isn't the important part. It could be anything—a spoon. A gold coin. It just happens to be a shell. Sadly, it's not very much. I have to make sure it lasts." I reached for it, and she put her hand over it. "I don't think you should touch it. It's powered."

"So your money actually does something?"

She looked confused. "Doesn't yours?"

Everything I knew about money was from what

I picked up from my high school boyfriend who was obsessed with Isaac Newton, and he wasn't cute enough for me to pay attention. (My boyfriend, not Isaac Newton.) Plus, I was probably almost definitely super high at the time. All I could remember was Isaac Newton's epic battle against coin shaving, and how he invented modern minting. (Hey, nice remembering, 10th grade stoner Ruby!)

"No," I told her. "Our money is a sort of stand in for the actual stuff that has value, which is locked up in a vault in the Midwest someplace. We all just collectively pretend it's worth something."

"A vault?" She suppressed a smile and asked, wide-eyed, "Is it guarded by a dragon?"

"You think I'm making this up!"

"It's fine. Mortals have the curse of dissembling, you can't help yourselves." She slipped the shell into her pocket, and made a pen out of her finger, poised over her palm. "Now, tell me again about Taco Tuesday." She grinned. "Leave out the dragons."

Lauren was obsessed with the idea of dinner parties, and was desperate to have one. I think it was the idea of giving your friends the gift of a meal and an experience. It seemed like an everyday thing to me, but at her own court it would have granted her a huge amount of status. I had to stop giving her drinks on the house when I realized I was putting her in my debt. (I did it anyway.)

I don't know if she had human emotions or just acted like she did, but she seemed to sympathize when I talked about my absent friends.

"Unicorns are funny things," she said one day over lunch. "Easy to love, obvs. They'd always get a rose. But hard to get them to stick around." She tapped the side of her head. "They are differently brained. But you're saying he was also a mortal man? Not just man-shaped?" She consulted her palm. "After you rescued him?"

I nodded. "For about a week. He didn't have a chance to get used to it. Some parts were really good. He did like human food. And music. He loved—loves—music. The part that confused him was time. He couldn't quite get his head around the idea that the past and now are two different things."

"Well, I've heard that to them, it's all the same. Like they can dip in and out. It's all happening at once."

That lined up with what Dr. Bel had said. I smiled sadly. "So he probably doesn't miss me." To him, either we were still together, or, and this was honestly more likely, he didn't think of me at all. I was right in the middle of feeling sorry for myself when my fork jerked in my hand, impaling a slice of tomato. "Fine," I muttered, "whatever. I'll eat vegetables."

Lauren was busy writing on her hand and missed the Random Magic. She looked back up at me. "You're taking it really well. He sounds like a babe."

"He was a total babe."

"I'm sorry. Now you're sad. Would it be better or worse to talk about Marly instead?"

I laughed. "It's fine. I just miss them both."

"You know where she is?" I nodded. "Then you should talk to her," Lauren said. "I mean, she'll probably flip a table." She finished her coffee. "Don't be upset, though. That just means she cares."

I fought with her to pay the check, and this time I let her win. I'm glad I did, it made her happy.

5

It was a pretty hopping night. I hustled my ass off, but in a good way. The crowd was just shy of putting me in the weeds, the music flowed, everyone was in a good mood, the tip jar was overflowing. I felt my phone buzz in my back pocket a time or two, but I never had a chance to look at it. Anyway, I think it's kind of tacky when you're waiting for your beer and your bartender is busy scrolling away. So it was after closing when I finally caught my breath and pulled my phone out. I had two texts from Lauren:

> **RUBY GET OVER HERE! YOU HAVE TO SEE THIS!**

I laughed. I could hear her breathless delivery. An

hour later, another:

> **SO COOL YOU WON'T BELIEVE IT I'LL WAIT UP**

By the time we got the bar closed and I was able to call an Uber, it was close to 3am. I hoped she was still awake.

The apartment was the same as ever from the outside; garbage tossed up against the chain link fence around the property, the windows sealed with sheet metal, the front doors boarded over and padlocked. I went through the narrow alley to the entrance, and as Shanti taught me, blew in my palm and placed it at the center of the brick wall. The garden path, the blooming trees, the columns and the sconces reappeared, and the troll opened the door for me. It was nice to be wanted.

The hallways were pretty empty at that hour, but not completely. What appeared to be a giant hedgehog tipped his hat to me on his way out of the elevator.

I got off at her floor—*thistle*—and wrinkled my nose at the smell. I guess Tha didn't get a chance to yell at Lauren's neighbor about taking care of their catbox. When I knocked on Lauren's door, it swung open. It was dark inside. I've watched enough CSI to know that is never a good thing. I got my garlic spray out and flipped the light on.

"Lauren? Honey, are you okay?" I headed towards

the bedroom, but stopped in my tracks when I saw the spreading pool of champagne on the kitchen floor. It took a second for me to realize that while it was shimmery and golden, it wasn't champagne. It was blood—fae blood. Lauren's blood. She was on the floor, sprawled on her back on the tile, her hands around the narrow metal pipe shoved through her chest.

"Holy shit, oh my God." I knelt next to her, but I didn't know if the fae had pulses, or whom to call, or what to do.

"Step away from her." I turned, and the next thing I knew my feet were two inches off the floor, and a fist was around my throat. My assailant was tall, and his eyes were black, no white at all. I could see light shimmering inside, like deep underwater. He was expressionless and his gloved hand was ice cold. The gloves were black with plates of black metal sewn into them, they went in ridged spirals up his arm. There was a dragon/cloud/tree insignia carved into the leather armor on his chest. It's funny what you notice. "Why did you murder our sister?"

"I didn't kill her," I squeaked.

"It doesn't matter," the man said. "You are responsible and so you are coming with me." That was when my random magic happened. The dishes in the sink rose into the air and crashed back down all at once. The man, startled, lowered his arm. My feet hit the floor, and I remembered I was holding my garlic spray. I blasted him right in those inky eyes. He blinked, licked his lips, and laughed.

"Piquant."

"Whuh...who are you?" That spray could take down a semi-truck, and he acted like it was water. For good measure, and because I seemed to have his attention, I repeated in a breathless bleat, "I didn't kill Lauren. She was my friend."

He raised a brow. "We fae don't make friends of your kind. She was here because of you, and so you must balance the scales."

The fucking scales again. March had been obsessed with the idea of justice being a literal scale—one-for-one—and it nearly got both of us killed. This man, I guessed he was also some sort of fae, must have gone to the same lecture.

"Let her go!" After that, things got sort of blurry, and not only because of the lack of blood going to my brain. The small room was filled with the hot smell of hunting, bronze feathers, and the roar of the harpy. Shanti, the harpy, my friend.

"This human is bound to La Belle Dame, and under her protection. And mine." Shanti— where the fuck she came from, I don't know—was perched with her hind feet (the eagle claws) on the stove and her front feet (the human-ish ones, more claws) on the breakfast bar. Her wings brushed the walls. Her Roman statue face was contorted in a snarl. I love her, but I was glad she wasn't coming after me. When she spoke, her mouth moved, but not in time to the words. Then she smiled, which was somehow worse, the expression never coming near her wild, marigold eyes. "I thought I smelled dark fae. What brings you so far from the Unseelie Court?"

The Unseelie Court. Okay. Well then. This was bad and getting worse.

The man released me and I collapsed onto the couch. "I think he's here because of Lauren." I pointed at the body, which was directly under her feathered belly.

"Shit! Oh no, we were going to go for pedis on Saturday." Shanti hopped herself forward so that all fours were on the bar, and with a fluff of her wings, transformed back to her human form. She materialized with her ankles primly crossed, wearing a plum knit dress that made her skin glow, and vintage Candy's. The girl was a thrift store savant. The man began to speak, and she held up an imperious hand. While we watched, she pulled the scrunchie out of her long, black hair, rummaged in her purse, and reapplied her lip gloss. "Now," she said to the man. "What's your name?"

He looked disgusted, but opened his mouth to tell her. Instead of colors and bells, it was a blast of black smoke and the sound of metal being demolished. Maybe a car door being torn in half.

Shanti rolled her eyes. "I obviously don't speak fae."

"Well," he sneered, "I *obviously* don't have a mortal name. I'm here for her." He jerked his head in my direction. "And for our sister. The scales—"

"Must be balanced, yes, I know. But she was from the Seelie Court. You're not. What business is this to you?" If it turned out I needed a lawyer, I was definitely hiring Shanti.

"Them? Those boiled plums couldn't find a feather in a high wind." None of that made a lick of sense. He continued. "When something goes awry they call on us. And something has obviously gone very awry." This guy liked to make a speech, I was getting that much. "And when something goes this wrong, the Seelie Court petitions the king to find justice. That's me. I am the king's justice."

"But don't you care that someone else killed her?" I asked. He turned those crazy black eyes back to me, and I was sorry I reminded him I was there.

"There is little difference between mortals. As I said, she was here because of you, and so you must come with me and serve the fae." He reached his gloved hand towards me again.

Well, that was a new element. I had a feeling serving the Unseelie king wasn't going to be making him a perfect Manhattan twice a week. "Wait!" He and Shanti both looked at me. "Scales. Of justice. Right?"

He nodded. Shanti cocked her head, waiting to see what I could come up with. Her eyes flashed orange and I looked at the deep gouges her claws left on the counter, and was glad we still had a Plan B.

"Well, so, if you take me, sure. Justice is served right now. But. Um. So, the person who actually killed Lauren is still out there. And they've killed one of the fae, which means they're probably really dangerous. They might kill again."

The man shrugged. "A problem for another day. And for the mortal authorities. What you do to each other is of no importance—"

Shanti picked up my idea and ran with it. "Well, certainly, they could kill mortals. Anyone can do that. And mortals killing each other is nothing to our kind. But could a mortal kill your sister fae so easily? I wonder. And would they stop at the murder of just one of you? No, perhaps they would not. And who didn't stop them? What kind of justice lets the killer of an innocent fae walk free to do it again? What would your king think of his justice now?"

He fussed with the shiny black leather of his gloves and looked away.

"When did you arrive? Did you even check to see if she was dead?" Shanti asked. She was into it.

"I didn't...um, a while ago, I don't know." He seemed flustered for the first time. Then he gathered himself. "I don't bother with the vagaries of your time—"

"So you sat here in the dark with your metal thumb up your ass, with poor Lauren dead on the floor while the *actual* killer got away?" He didn't reply, but he did open and close his mouth a few times. Shanti continued. "Your king will be mega pissed to hear you blew the chance to catch the real killer. Twice." I put her in charge of all future closing arguments.

The man sighed. He crossed his arms. His leathery looking armor squeaked as he moved. Like his gloves, it was black and had the sheen of oil on water. So did his long, long hair. "You make a point. I'll have to bring this before the king. Do not touch the body of our sister, and do not think to flee." Then he was gone.

6

As soon as I was sure he was gone, I jumped up and threw my arms around Shanti. "Holy Christ, it's good to see you. How did you find me?"

She got a little shifty eyed. "I was in the neighborhood?" I gave her a look and she sighed. "You may not like it. Dr. Bel asked me to keep an eye on you."

I know she was expecting me to blow up at her, but what was a little stalking among friends? "What, you think I'm gonna be mad at you? I'm sorry, honey, this shouldn't be your job, to watch out for me. And I'm not even mad at Dr. Bel. I've just been busy."

"You haven't been to see her in months. Since..."

"Since I took her crap advice and came clean to Marly." I knelt next to Lauren again. "I know, I know. It wasn't crap advice. I'm just glad you showed up. Fae dude wasn't playing. I'd be long gone, and no one would know where I went." I shuddered. "I think you saved my life." I gently brushed Lauren's hair back from her brow. "I wish we could have helped her. She texted me, a couple of hours ago. She said she had something to tell me. I wish I'd gotten here earlier."

"Then you'd both be dead, and fae dude would have tried to snatch me, since I would have come looking for you." She grinned and her dark eyes bloomed in orange. "That would have been a fight. Never seen an Unseelie fae before. They're even bigger snobs than the Seelie folk." She paused. "Kind of hot, though."

She wasn't wrong. I let that go without comment. "What did he mean by 'serve the king'? Do you know?"

She helped me pull a pink and white knitted afghan off the couch and arrange it over Lauren. "No idea, and let's not find out." She straightened up and put her hands on her hips. "Should we wait for him to come back?"

"I'm thinking yes. I don't want him showing up at my house, or the bar. I hope it doesn't take too long. Do they have time dilation or something in fairy land?" The adrenaline rush of finding Lauren and getting mauled by the fae dude was starting to burn out, and I was wiped. I couldn't stop looking at the slowly spreading pool of sparkling blood, and the tips of Lauren's fingers sticking out from under the blanket. The pretty green polish had flaked away and there was something stringy caked under her torn fingernails.

Shanti sat next to me. She looked pretty tired, too. "What made you come here in the first place? What did she say on the phone?"

"She actually texted me. She was freaking out about something, but not in a bad way, and said I had to see something. That was..." I checked my phone. "About three hours ago. Look." I passed it to Shanti. "I guess whoever killed her did it just after that. And then dude showed up. So the shuttle service between here and the Unseelie Court is pretty quick." I paused. "You don't have to wait with me..."

Thank god she just laughed. "Doctor Bel would pull off my wings. I want to call her and fill her in. Is that okay?" I nodded and she went into the hallway. I could hear her lilting South Asian accent and leaned my head back. I'd just close my eyes for a second...

"I blame you for all of this." I snapped my head up, and fae dude was looming over me. His hand was on the hilt of his knife, which, since it looked as long as my arm, was thankfully still in its sheath. At his feet was a big duffle bag. Like everything else, it was black and shiny. I wondered if the Unseelie all dressed like it was fetish night at the club, or if it was just him. "You are responsible." I scuttled backwards against the couch, but he sighed and turned away. He drew off his leather and metal gloves and tossed them in his bag, and then knelt and pulled the quilt off of Lauren.

"What are you doing?" Shanti demanded. "I thought your king was going to send a proper investigator."

He glanced over his shoulder at her. "Oh, the king agreed with you. He was delighted to hear from one of your kind. He loves harpies. He wishes to extend an invitation for you to visit the court at your convenience. He says you two shall have a glorious hunt."

She nodded. "I will consider his offer. But why are—"

"The king agrees with everything you said, particularly that I nearly took the wrong creature back to my court. That the killer of our sister slipped out of my grasp."

"Well you didn't have to tell him all of that!" she said.

He stared at her. I could see silvery lights swimming in his eyes. "The king knows everything that happened here. Including everything you said. If you know anything about us..."

"You had to tell him everything." She nodded, and turned to me. "That's what I was saying. They can't lie."

"Oh, and I was also reprimanded for finding excuses to go back to the court rather than continue this assignment."

"That doesn't seem fair," I said. "You're totally doing your job."

He sighed and for a second his glare faded. He just looked sad. "The king is...he can be capricious. Once he has given an order or made a ruling, he strongly prefers not to revisit the case. His hand was forced, what with my going back home without this being resolved. The king is correct—since I already know the particulars, I am to find her killer." He shook his dark head. "That doesn't make this any less of a nightmare. I never do this part." He looked over at us, both on the couch. "I don't suppose you know who did this to her? Any ideas? No, that would be too easy. Well." We watched him carefully lift Lauren off the floor, and then arrange her body on the dinner table, placing her arms at her sides. I noticed the palms of her hands and the insides of her wrists were red and blistered. The table was too short for even her petite frame, and her feet flopped off the edge. Poor thing, she'd never have her dinner party.

Once the fae had wiped the frothy golden blood off his hands, he leaned over Lauren, and with his thumb pulled her lower eyelid down. "Do you have good water?" Shanti went to the kitchen, carefully stepping over the blood, and got a tumbler of tap water. "I said good water." Even though Shanti handed it to him, he glared at me like I'd spat in the glass.

"Anacostia's finest," I said. "Although I wouldn't necessarily drink it. What's it for?"

He ignored me, and I watched as he delicately pinched the white of her eye and pulled out a flat, shiny creature which squirmed in his fingers. It was brownish and see-through, it looked a bit like a piece of old-fashioned filmstrip with tiny legs flailing in each corner. He dropped it in the glass, and repeated the procedure on her other eye. Both her eyes were now solidly black. He lifted the glass and watched the two little square animals swim around. I don't know what I was expecting, but after a minute he swallowed the water and both creatures in a gulp. Then he closed his eyes and a shadow—pain, maybe? —crossed his face. When he reopened his eyes, they were nearly human. Like Lauren's, they were green. His were darker than hers, and far less friendly. If it was supposed to help him pass as human, I guess it was a start. He'd probably need to work on the swirling, hip length hair, and the blue cast to his pale skin. He looked like something painted on the side of a van.

He opened the big duffel bag he'd brought with him, and pulled out a couple of paper bags. Then he took Lauren's hands and put them inside, securing them at the wrist like brown paper mittens.

"Are those magic rubber bands?" I asked.

He looked over his shoulder at me. "That is not a thing. Please stop speaking."

"But what are they for?"

I got another look of disgust, but he said, "If the killer left a trace of themselves behind, the bags will collect it," he said. "Given some time, those traces will grow and become visible."

"Like, from under her nails? Like a DNA test?"

He paused and stared at me. "If I say yes, will you stop talking?"

Then he went over her body, I guess looking for clues. I was struck by the respectful way he treated her. He was gentle, turning her head from side to side and arranging her blouse around the horrible wound in her chest. "I suppose we don't have to wonder what killed her." The metal bar looked like it went right through her heart. "She fought back, though. Our sister was brave."

"How do you know she fought back?"

"Her hands were burned. By the iron." So that's what the marks were; scorch marks. She must have tried to wrestle it away from the person who killed her, or maybe even pull it out. I felt sick. Poor Lauren.

"So," he concluded, "her attacker was not one of the fae." I noticed how careful he was not to touch the metal bar.

"Or they wore gloves," I added, trying to be helpful. Then I leaned forward on the couch. "It looks like the person who did this was much taller than she was. Look at the angle." All those CSI reruns were finally paying off. The man nodded, and I felt like I scored a point.

"Hey, where's her phone?" said Shanti. "We should see if there are any texts or anything."

The man rose to his feet. "She lived like a mortal, with mortal things. I'll need to see her possessions. This place must be kept secure." He fished around in the bag again, and handed me a thick gold coin inscribed with the same dragon/cloud that was on his chest, and something that looked like a business card, except I think it was made of bone. It had writing on it, but nothing I could read. "Do you accept these tokens?"

The way he said it should have tipped me off, but tonight had been a lot. I nodded.

"Good. Please give this to the one who manages this place. Let no one come inside. Then go home, mortal woman." He looked at Shanti. "You, too. I'll have to take our sister home and report what I know. I'm certain I will not be received with a banquet. I'll return and I will look for you."

He carefully pulled the paper bags off her ruined, burned hands and securing them with the non-magical rubber bands, he put both bags in the fridge. Then he wrapped Lauren's body in the quilt. I could just see the top of her head—dark tufts sticking up through the blanket. I hadn't known her very long, but I'd liked her. I wished her well. "I'll be waiting for your call," I told the man. He took a step towards me, and with another, he disappeared.

7

Shanti and I thought about sharing a cab, but since she was going to Shaw and I was going to Columbia Heights, it didn't make sense. She made me swear I'd go straight home and text her when I got there. I took a last look around the now-quiet apartment. The blood remained on the kitchen floor, and with the only light coming in from the hallway, it looked black and oily. Lauren was gone, and I had one more job before I could go home—deliver the coin and the card. I hoped Tha would be awake.

I shut the door to Lauren's place, but didn't lock it—I didn't know where the key was, and honestly didn't want the responsibility. I could only think of what happened to Marly when she was in charge of my keys. I headed for the elevator, and the tall, weeping woman came around the corner. She gracefully inclined her impossibly long neck towards me as we passed, and I felt the spider web edge of one of her unraveling lace veils brush my arm...

...and then my legs went out from under me and I was on the ground. I wrapped my arms around my head and my body convulsed with the force of my sobs. A cloud of stink rose from my ridiculous, useless body. I brought misery and suffering wherever I went. I'd never been loved, only used. The world wouldn't notice if I died, in fact, the only question was how to make it fast...

It stopped. The veiled woman stood over me, holding the lace that had snagged on my backpack when she passed me.

"Sorry about that," she said. "You'll be fine in a jiff. Have a nice night."

I pulled myself upright and sat with my back against the wall next to the elevator and took a deep, shuddering breath. She was right, I was fine. What must it be like, walking around with all that power? What was she? I thought again about all the xenos I'd invited into my life. I needed to be more careful.

When I was sure the horrible cloud had lifted, I went to look for Tha. I was happy to see she was in her office with the door open, reading a copy of *Vogue* in a language I don't speak. I knocked and she looked up.

"You're here late, human lady," she observed.

"Did you know what happened tonight? To Lauren?" She did not. "She's dead. I mean, someone killed her."

Her eyes widened, then narrowed. I think she suspected I had something to do with it, at least at first. She peppered me with questions: did I smell anything unusual? That one gave me pause. Was a vampire involved? The same one that took Marly? I struggled to remember, but finally had to admit that, no, nothing in her apartment smelled strange. She asked about Lauren's body, and I tried to be as precise as possible. Burned hands and wrists, iron bar. Yes, a struggle. No, her door was unlocked when I got there. And then I told her about the Unseelie fae. As I described the scene, it got harder to see her. I finally realized it was because she was smoking. Or something was—in any case, her little office was filling with billowing fragrant smoke. Was it incense? My eyes were starting to tear up, and when I got to the part about the fae king demanding that I serve him, a huge brass and scarlet shadow rose behind her. The shadow spiraled and coiled around where Tha was sitting, and finally she was completely obscured. Then she was the shadow, and her office and the hotel itself seemed to melt away until there was nothing but the dragon, I could only see parts of her, the rest disappeared into—I don't know. Somewhere else. Her head was massive, the sinuous neck didn't look strong enough to hold it up, and her body shimmered with heat. Drips and blobs of gold leaked from between the scales along her side and pooled on the carpet.

Her glossy black wings remained folded alongside the sharp, raised ridges of her spine. If she opened them, she would have taken out the walls. Her enormous eyes—brilliant copper veined with leaf green—slowly blinked as she watched me talk.

I did my best to keep going and not wet myself. When I pulled out the coin and the card, they fell out of my shaking hands onto the desk. She bowed her head at the end of that gleaming neck, and blew a jet of sweet-smelling smoke across the room. Then the smoke and the shadows and the dragon collapsed back in on themselves, and she was Tha again. She picked the card up, and when she turned it over in her hands it became a smooth jade disc. Like the card, it was covered with writing, incised in the surface. Like the card and her magazine, I couldn't read it.

"In my house," she said. Her voice shook with anger. "This is not done." She tapped a slender finger on the coin, and set the disc down between us. "Tell the Unseelie fae he may count on my cooperation. I myself will guarantee Miss Lauren's room is undisturbed. He may use it as he sees fit."

"Thank you—"

"On one condition. The fae will turn the assassin over to me." She folded her hands around the jade disc.

"I think he's supposed to bring them back to his king—"

"To me," she repeated. "I have a reputation to

maintain." She held out her hand. "Give me your phone." I handed it over and she entered her number into my contacts. Her avatar was a pink and purple cartoon dragon.

"This is cute," I said.

That got me a rare smile. "My grandson picked it out." Then she got serious again. "Don't worry about the king. You find anything, you let me know."

I shoved it into my bag and wearily said I'd let the king know what she said. The two of them could hash it out. "Your driver is outside," she said. "Do not embarrass him by attempting to pay him." She slipped the coin into a drawer in her desk. "The Unseelie Court is generous when it comes to their servants."

"What? I'm not a servant."

"You accepted these tokens, didn't you? You are in the service of the Unseelie king."

Tokens. Gifts. I mentally slapped myself. Well, I'd try and sort it out after I got some sleep. I poured myself into the backseat of the Rav 4, and the driver turned the music up a bit. It was reggae, and I dozed in the back to the sound of him singing along about someone not wanting to wait in vain. When I opened my eyes, we were at my front gate. I reached for my wallet, and saw a concerned look cross his face as he watched me in the rearview mirror. I covered by pulling my keys out of my backpack, and was rewarded by the man's gorgeous smile.

Although I hated to do it, I called Claudio and filled him in on the whole night. We both cried a little bit, and agreed we'd help the Unseelie fae.

"Justice for Lauren," he said, "and I want to meet your leather daddy."

"He's not my—"

"I know, fool. Go to sleep."

I left out the part about the dragon, I was so tired I figured it was even odds I might have dreamt her up. For my last act, I shot Shanti a quick text that I'd made it home in one piece. By the time I crawled into bed, the sun was coming through the blinds. Even by my standards, the night had been a lot: Lauren was dead, the spooky but hot male fae had shown up, I met a dragon, and I was on the payroll of the Unseelie king.

"I have to find her phone," I said out loud, and then I was asleep.

8

The next day was quiet, for which I was grateful. My phone didn't ring, no one dropped from the sky, no one got murdered and my interactions were xeno-free (as far as I knew, anyway). Not getting out of bed until 3 p.m. is the main ingredient for a stress-free life. But, I was about to find out there were more dangerous things than xenos out there. Yeah, I'm talking middle-schoolers.

It was my turn to open the bar, so I was alone, polishing the bottles, slicing limes and stacking glasses. I didn't hear the door open.

"You Ruby?" That question again!

I looked up. Two kids were standing in the doorway. "You guys, this is a bar. The restaurant is downstairs." The pair—a boy and a girl—looked too young to be up here. He had scraggly chin-whiskers and the hair I could see under the girl's knit cap looked like it had been dyed with pink Kool-Aid. She wore a rubber choker, neon pink to match. God, were those things back? I'm terrible at telling ages but I guessed they were around thirteen. "Anyway, we don't open for another half an hour."

They didn't leave, just gave each other a series of wide-eyed looks. One of them was going to have to approach the bar. My money was on the boy. The girl, with her cap pulled down and the sleeves of her hoodie yanked over her hands, was just about folding herself in half to avoid being noticed. Not that I would know anything about that sort of behavior. Sure enough, the boy took a step towards me.

"I'm Ray. This is Sheena. You're Ruby?"

"Yeah. Why are you asking?" I set the rag down and came out to lean against the bar rail.

"We're in Ms. Gonzales' class." He held up his phone. "This is you, right?"

He had it open to Instagram, and it was Marly's page—although it hadn't been updated since spring. It was a selfie of the two of us out on U Street, going to dinner. She wore the necklace I got her from a vacation in the Florida Keys and a huge grin and towered over me as usual. I think it was the last time we did anything together. No, I know it was. "Yeah, that's me. Marly—um, Ms. Gonzales is your teacher?"

"She was," said the girl—Sheena. "She's been

missing for weeks. Have you seen her?"

I hadn't seen her, but I didn't know she was blowing off work. I could say that's when I got worried, but the truth was I'd been worried for a long time, even before Claudio told me about his sightings. I tried to figure out what to say that wouldn't freak out these two amateur detectives. "Why do you think she's missing? Are you sure she didn't just go on vacation?"

"We were in the middle of The Martian Chronicles," said Sheena, like that explained everything.

"Yeah, and?" I asked.

Sheena looked at me like I had just farted in class. "You don't just leave during Bradbury."

"You're her friend," said Ray, obviously trying to get the interrogation back on track. "She didn't say anything to you?"

"No," I said, and at least that was true. "I haven't talked to her for a while."

"You have a fight?" Ray was giving me the eye like I was in the box and maybe ought to lawyer up.

"We just lost touch," I told him. Again, that was true.

"Maybe you ought to go see her, get back in touch" Ray said.

Sheena nodded in agreement. "Tell her third period English misses her."

The door opened again. Claudio took out his earbuds and tossed his backpack on the bar.

"Are these the new bartenders?"

"Nah man, we were just leaving." Ray turned back to me, and then fiddled with his phone. "If you hear anything, catch me on Brilo. I'm sending you a code, bro." Ray nodded solemnly at me and then Claudio, and jerked his head at Sheena, who followed him out.

As she left, she turned and gave me a worried look. "Tell her to come back, okay? The sub sucks."

They clomped down the steps. I sighed and crossed my arms. "Clo?"

"Yeah, bro?"

"What's Brillo?" When he was done laughing at me, he took my phone and downloaded the app.

"You gonna go see her?"

"I think I have to try. If they found me, who knows who else they'll go looking for?" Not all xenos were sweet like March or kind like Dr. Bel. Even Shanti, if you caught her on a bad day, could be dangerous. And then there were things like that nasty fox creature—the *kitsune* that March and I talked to in the woods last year. No, best to get them to back off. What I had to do now was to figure out how to reassure them their favorite teacher was just taking a little break. There wasn't any way around it. Lauren, Dr. Bel, Claudio—everyone had it right. I just had to talk to her. If she told me to get lost, at least I could tell the kids I tried. I didn't want to brush them off, but I sure wasn't going to tell them their teacher was suffering vampire PTSD. If that's what it was.

The regulars came and went like the tide, Claudio and I did shots in Lauren's honor, and kept the magic of our partnership alive with an ice throwing contest (he won, having clocked me in the head with ice cubes a record eight out of ten times.) The back of my mind was busy wondering when the Unseelie fae would reappear, and what I'd have to do to get out of going home with him on a permanent vacation. The front of my mind was worrying about Marly, like usual. Midnight grocery runs were one thing, but I know Marly loved those kids, and she wouldn't have simply left them without an explanation. If she wouldn't let me in, I could stand in the street and yell at the window. Tomorrow, I decided. I'd at least do a drive-by.

"The king requires that you call me Chad," said the Unseelie fae. I swear I'd looked in that direction not ten seconds before, so he must have chosen just that moment to materialize at the end of the bar. It looked like he had a movie-montage makeover back in Unseelie land, because instead of goth-y leather armor, he wore a simple black blazer and a white, collarless button down. His black mailed gloves were switched out for thin, black driving gloves. He wore a dull silver medallion with the dragon/cloud/thing on a leather cord, and his skin was pale, not pale blue. His hair was no longer waist length, just very black. The only thing separating him from a regulation white guy with an expensive haircut were the tiny creature contact lenses which made the irises of his dark green eyes just a bit too large.

"That is an interesting opening line," said Claudio, leaning on the bar. "How's it work out for you?"

I gritted my teeth and made some introductions. "Claudio, this is the representative of the Unseelie Court we talked about. Remember?"

"I am here," the Unseelie fae said, "to bring the killer of our sister to justice. I'm usually just in charge of punishment, so this mortal woman will be assisting my investigation."

"Cool story," said Claudio. "But no one is calling you Chad."

The fae looked surprised. "The king has carefully researched human behavior. There is a gathering at the sea where the chosen ones fornicate. The most perfect of them was Chad, and so am I to be."

"I think they're watching *Bachelors in Paradise* over there," I told Claudio. To the Unseelie fae I said, "Not going to happen."

"Nope," agreed Claudio.

"Chad is the worst."

Now the fae looked indignant. "I am the worst."

"Aw, come on. Don't be down on yourself like that." I felt like Claudio was making a friend, which was nice?

"I am the worst," he repeated, "when I bring justice to the wicked and unworthy. I am the worst, and last thing they see. You must call me Chad."

Claudio and I looked at each other. "It won't come out of my mouth," he said. "How about Sasha?"

I leaned over and quietly asked, "Where did you get that from?"

"Ru Paul," he whispered back. More loudly, he said "Sasha is a great warrior and a fierce competitor. A champion. You can tell your boss it's the nickname for Chad."

The fae shrugged. "Fine. Hopefully I won't need it for long." He gave a critical look around the bar. "It smells, it's dark, and there's something on this wood that feels unpleasant under my hand."

"Ah," Claudio said, "you've looked us up on Yelp. Want a drink?"

The Unseelie fae—Sasha—glared at Claudio. Honestly, I think 'glare' was his default. "The last time I drank my glass overflowed with the blood of black roses, the finest—" Claudio handed him a gin and tonic. "...actually, this is not bad."

"Sorry we don't stock rose blood," Claudio said.

A young woman pulled up to the bar and waved me over. "Are you Ruby?" She looked to be a regular human for a change—not that I could one hundred percent tell, of course. I made a note to eventually stop answering that question, but I told her I was.

"Some guy downstairs wants to talk to you."

"Is it a kid?" I didn't think Ray would be back that

late. Didn't kids have curfews?

"What? No, it's a full-on grown cute dude."

I looked over at Claudio. "Could be your fan club," he said. "Don't they meet on Thursday nights?" Helpful as usual.

"Girl, you have to go see him. Like, just go." Her eyes were wide. "He's an absolute babe!"

It can't be. It isn't. Don't get excited. It won't be him.

"Well, go on," Claudio flapped a dishrag at me. "It's dead in here anyway. I'll entertain his lordship." He turned away. "So what's this I'm hearing about some sweet leather gear?"

I went downstairs and peeked through the French doors at the empty dining room of The Tortoise. Service had finished a few hours ago and the staff had all gone home. Lights were on in the kitchen—those guys job is literally never done—but no one would be waiting for me back there. The patio was also dark, the umbrellas tied up and the chairs flipped onto the tables. I looked around the corner, down the cobbled path that led to the tiny back garden, and there he was, leaning against the wall. The streetlight caught him in a glowing cone of yellow, but I think my unicorn came equipped with his own light.

So, what to do? Play it cool? Leap on top of him? Cry? I just stood there, shaking, feeling my dumb pink Valentine's Day balloon heart pound for the first time in months. I stood there, within reach if he wanted.

He looked exactly the same; tall, tan (an all-over tan, a golden body, that ass...) longish dark hair, and the holdover that marked him as being what he really was—a shock of silvery hair falling over his left eye.

"You look exactly the same," he said.

I smiled. "It hasn't been that long."

"No," he replied, "it has been very long. It has been eight months and sixteen days, and whatever time it is. It has been a very long time."

Time. Time and memory. I quit smiling. "Should you know that?"

He shook his head. "But I do. I've been thinking about you." I couldn't help but notice he didn't look exactly happy about it. "I've been remembering you. I've been worrying about you." He reached out and circled my wrist. "I put myself back into this body. I swore I'd never do it again. But no matter the body I live in, it didn't matter. I couldn't stop thinking about you. In my real body, I couldn't protect you. I couldn't do this." His fingers tightened and he gave the barest tug, just a gentle pull, and that was all it took. I forgot my anger, my regret, the guilt, the fear—I forgot everything but the heat in his kisses, and his arms around me. My feet left the ground like someone had turned off gravity as he lifted and pulled me close, and I wrapped my legs around his hips. The silver streak in his hair fell across my eyes and the world turned bright.

"So is this how it's going to be?" I asked, coming up

for a breath. "You'll just appear?"

"I don't have a phone," he reminded me, setting me back on my feet, "or else I would have sent you a text." He had a point. "I could leave," he added, looking innocently at the sky, "and then come back when you're ready. I could send a letter, if I had a stamp."

"Fine," I laughed. "You'll just appear. I'm happy you did. I've missed you, too." I could see he wanted to talk about that, about time and memory, but his hands had found their way under my blouse, and my own hands slid inside the back of his jeans, and we had some things to take care of before we could have a chat. I gently pulled free.

"Can we go to your house?" he asked. "Do you still have a house?"

"Yeah, same place. Come up with me, say hi to Claudio, and I'll get my bag. Then we can go, okay?" It was a good plan, but I was forgetting something.

9

I led March back up the stairs, and called out to Claudio, "Look who—-" but instead of the bar, I found myself...somewhere else. Outside, but not on Earth. Someplace vast. Someplace dark. A high-pitched whining sound made my teeth ache, and the air smelled like scorched oil. The blue-black sky tore itself apart with constant lightning, but there was no thunder, just that whining buzz. I dropped to my hands and knees on dead grass and tried to get my bearings. In the flickering, strobing light from the sky I could see March off in the distance, standing in a lighted rectangle. The doorway? To the bar? I turned and saw the dark fae—Sasha—at the other end of the open space. It was like a football field ringed by dead trees, with the two of them at either end, and me somehow dropped onto the 50-yard line. What was beyond the ring of flattened grass and skeleton trees I had no idea, but the lumped outlines of mountains were moving. I don't know how I knew it, but they were watching. And they thought this was amusing and interesting. The two of them had the mountains' attention, and all I wanted to do was hide—lay flat on the grass and put my hands over my head until they turned away. Instead, I shakily got my feet under me, which caught the eye of something else. Whatever it was flew past me, striking my shoulder with a wet, pulpy wing that was more of a tentacle. I couldn't see it—I couldn't see all of it at once, but what I caught glimpses of in the uneven light was darker than black and it pulsed and rippled as it moved. It flew over and around me, stroking me with its parts as it passed. It left damp, sticky trails on my jacket and smelled like low tide. I screamed and batted at it, and my hands passed through a bunch of its 'arms'. They felt like wrist-thick overcooked noodles, and dropped, writhing, at my feet before melting into the now-muddy grass.

"Ow," it wailed in a child's voice, "you hurt me! You're bad and I'm telling!"

It darted away crying, saying I was going to be in trouble. I wiped my wet hands on my ruined jacket, glad I couldn't quite see what clung to them. I didn't know who or what it was going to 'tell' but I didn't want to hang around and find out.

The humming in my head grew from a whine to a shriek, and I tried to call to March, but my voice died in the stinking air. I had a sickening flash of Baba Yaga's hut, of roses and knives, and stumbled back towards the light. It was my plan to get back to the door, but March wasn't there anymore. Well, he was, but it wasn't March, the man I'd just been kissing. Whatever this place was, it must have freed his real form—not the graceful white horse, not my strange and beautiful lover, but his truly otherworldly self. He looked like living lightning. He rose up, and I could see the air crackle and sizzle around him. He smashed back down against the ground, and part of his white flame flew straight at me. I dove out of the way but not fast enough; I got knocked over, flattened, and tossed backwards; it felt like a wave crashing me onto the beach. Sasha—his intended target, of course, was just as changed. His black armor was a live thing, his hair writhed around him, he was a shining ebony blade. He countered March's attack with one of his own, and this time I got thrown against something hard I couldn't see. I clutched whatever it was—thin bars or spindles—and tensed for the next round. When March struck, this time it flew over my head, and I watched as Sasha bent himself out of the way. It wasn't a move you could make with normal physics, and it hurt to look at. Even though the light weapon missed me, it felt like a huge fist squeezing my head, and then letting go, and that hurt even worse. It was hard to see to begin with, and the pressure was doing something to the insides of my eyes. The pain was ramping up, I had to get the two of them to stop, but I couldn't get off the ground. Blinking away tears, I raised my head. They were poised to attack again, and if I wasn't about to get squashed, I would have spent more time noticing how gorgeous, how un-human they both looked. Light and dark chess pieces. They fired.

Oh, shit.

The blasts of energy raced in my direction from both sides, I could feel the rippling waves of pressure trying to tear my head open, and I screamed.

The noise stopped. At least, the whining buzz stopped. The normal background bar noise— the stereo, the customers, traffic—that all came back. I was on the floor, huddled against the bar and clinging to a barstool. Apparently, that's what I'd been hanging on to. March and Sasha, now turned back to a couple of men—excuse me—a couple of assholes who just about killed me, were standing over me, glaring at each other. I climbed the rungs of the barstool to get back to my feet, slapping March's hand away. I took a deep breath and looked from one to the other.

"I don't know what kind of dick-measuring bullshit that was supposed to be, but it never happens again, am I clear?" Without waiting for an answer, I turned to Claudio. "What just happened?"

He passed me a glass of water. "You two—oh, hiiiiii, March—you guys walked in, and then you fell on the floor." His eyes widened. "Did you have a stroke? Can smile?"

"No, I can't goddamn smile." Before I took a sip of water—I was desperately thirsty—I stripped off my soggy jacket and threw it into the trash can behind the bar. I wondered if I ought to burn it. Once I gulped down half the glass, I looked in the mirror behind the bar and squinted at my reflection. "Oh, perfect," I said. I wiped moisture off my face and held out my hand. "A bloody nose. Thank you very much, now I have a brain tumor."

Sasha leaned forward and put two fingers under my chin. He turned my head from side to side. "Your brain is undamaged. But you have a tooth going bad. Upper right, halfway back. You're welcome."

"Gross. And hands off, okay?" I wiped my nose with a bar nap.

Sasha jerked his chin at March and asked, "What is *that* doing here? Do you get a lot of unicorns?"

"Sure," I told him. "They come rolling in great herds off the tundra, oh, no wait, that's caribou."

"Ruby," said March, in his slow, sweet voice. "Who's your friend?"

10

As much as I wanted to shoot balls of flame at both of them, I managed to press 'pause' on my rage stroke. Once again, it was time for introductions. At this rate I was going to have to get name tags made up. While they stood with their arms folded, glaring at each other, I did my best to sum up the last few months. "...and then tonight Sasha showed back up here, looking all human."

He smiled at me, I think for the first time. "Do you think?"

"Oh yeah, you're giving me trust-fund-metrosexual-realness with just a touch of MMA."

He gave me a brief blank look. I'd bet my second home and my stock portfolio he had no idea what that meant. But he put that smile back on and said, "That is exactly what the king intended."

So,” said March, who was not smiling, “you’re to ke my Ruby as some sort of servant?”

My Ruby? I filed that one away, too. We’d have a lot to talk about, if we ever got out of this bar.

“Technically,” Sasha replied, “she is the servant of the king. She accepted the terms of her own free will.”

“I did?” That night at Lauren’s seemed a thousand years ago, not just a day. I remembered the gold coin and the card, and how I just took them without even thinking about it. I’d put myself in the Unseelie Court’s debt. Good move. “Oh, you mean when I took the coin. Yeah, I guess I did.”

“You accepted a gift from him?” March took me by the upper arm. “Would you all excuse us?” he said, and pulled me aside. “What were you thinking?” He raked back his long hair. “Well, it doesn’t matter. We have to figure out how to get...what was it? A coin? You have to return it to him. Oh, and you’ll have to tally everything you received from him, it all has to be repaid—”

“No, March. I’m not giving it back. I’m going to help him.”

He looked surprised. I admit, I was sort of surprised myself. “He’s dangerous,” he said.

I touched his hand with just the tips of my fingers. “You’re dangerous. I helped you.”

He shook his head and wrapped his hand around mine. “It’s not the same.” Then he raised his head and gave me a sharp look. “At least I hope it’s not.”

I yanked my hand away. "Oh my God, March, really?" This whole evening had gone utterly sideways. I took a deep breath. "Okay, listen. It's not like that. And I guess it's nice that you're concerned, but don't be. The main thing is he's here. He's supposed to find out what happened to Lauren, and I am going to help him. Not because of some coin, but because I liked her, and it's the right thing to do. Do you understand?"

He took my hand again. I guess he was thinking about it. Then he said, "Are you hurt? That dark place—you were not supposed to be there, shiny stone." he asked.

Despite myself, I smiled at the name and the way he oh-so subtly tried to change the subject. I bet nobody else's magical boyfriend called them a rock and meant it in a good way. Then I caught myself leaning towards him, wanting everything to be fine. I felt my anger draining away and did my best to keep a little bit of ire going, at least until I figured out what happened. The March Effect. "Well, thanks for noticing. What was that place?"

"It is for settling scores. For combat, as you saw. I issued the challenge when I saw the Unseelie fae, and he accepted. I don't know how you got pulled along. I would...I was about to say I would never put you in danger, but that's not true, is it?" He sighed. "I'm very sorry. It's obviously not a place for mortals."

"Other than being slimed by a giant flying baby

"I'm okay."

"A..."

"It had tentacles and I accidentally pulled one of its arms off. It started crying and went to tell its mother on me."

"Things grow large there. Very large. I think you probably shouldn't go back."

I thought of the mountains that weren't mountains, and the crawling feeling of being watched. "Fine with me. The place gave me a headache, and the squid gave me the creeps, but I'm feeling better. And I guess I don't have a brain tumor, so I've got that going for me." March reached under my hair and gently massaged the base of my skull. It felt like heaven and I let the last bit of anger float off. "Why did you challenge Sasha? How do you know him?"

He looked over my shoulder at the bar, I guess to see what his arch mortal enemy was up to. "Sasha. I do not know him. I know his king, though."

That got my attention. "Really? From where?"

"His king hunted me, once. Long ago." Long ago, which is different from yesterday, or now. I added it to what he'd said outside the bar. This was new, his ability to fix things in time.

"What happened?"

He smiled. "He did not catch me." March shot another look in the direction of the bar. "He wished to add me to his collection, and perhaps he still does.

You should keep a distance. The Unseelie fae are poor company." Then he looked back at me. "Would you like me to challenge him again? I'll leave you here this time, and I'll see he goes home in disgrace." At least they weren't trying to kill each other.

"No, please don't. If you do something to him, the king'll just send another one. And that one might be worse. Let him do his job, and then he'll leave."

"His job. With your assistance."

He was still on that, and I smiled. "You really are jealous."

He tried to pretend he was surprised I would even think such a thing. "Of him? No, I fear he'll drag you to a dark and dangerous place." The irony wasn't lost on me, but I let him continue. "The stain of him will be a blot on your beautiful self."

"You're worried about me." I had a lot to think about; even though I would love it to be true, I knew March hadn't just dropped back in because he missed me. He had changed in some fundamental way, and he obviously needed my help in figuring out what had happened to him. Sasha also needed me or Lauren's killer might never be caught, and I felt enough of a responsibility to her memory to not let that happen.

They both needed me, but it remained to be seen if they could be in the same room without burning each other down.

"Of course I am worried about you," he said. "You

are important."

"Important in like, a key to solving some mystery?" The mystery of time and memory, for instance?

He looked at me strangely. "You are important to me." Then he nodded, as if he'd come to a conclusion. "I will join you in your search for the killer of the Seelie fae woman. It'll go faster and he'll leave sooner."

"I think you'll have to run that past Sasha. He'll tell his king you're here, you know."

"Well, he may do that anyway. Perhaps he'll be grateful for the assistance and wait until his mission is over to betray me." He smiled like this was a cool plot twist. "Let's see."

I started to tell him I thought this was maybe a little reckless, but he was already on his way back to the bar, where Claudio was letting Sasha taste-test all the garnishes.

"Olives," Sasha was saying. "Clearly superior." He rose to his feet. "You're still here. Shall we continue?"

"Let's start over," March said. I just stood back and let it happen, whatever the hell it turned out to be. "I wish to assist you."

Sasha was clearly not expecting this. Neither was I, frankly. "You...just challenged me. On the Fields of Significant Contact."

"Is that what that place is called?" I asked. They ignored me.

"I withdraw my challenge. Your mission, to find

the killer of your kin, it's important?"

"I accept your withdrawal. Yes. And not only to me."

The air was charged between them. Even here on the regular, non-significant contact plane, I could see it crackle.

"Who comes up with the names?" I wondered aloud. "I mean, I figured it would be called, like The Labyrinth of Pain, or the Arena of Despair."

March glanced at me. "Did you hit your head after all?" Then he turned his attention back to Sasha. "You refer to your king. He'll want to know you've seen me. Will you tell him?"

Sasha looked uncomfortable. "The king is...I...I will not be going back to the Unseelie Court until this matter is resolved."

"Are you two in a fight?" asked Claudio. The two magical creatures turned to look at him. They'd forgotten he was there.

"We were literally on the field of battle ten minutes ago, what do you think?" asked Sasha.

Claudio gave him a look I recognized as You've Been Downgraded. "I meant you and your boyfriend the king."

"Oh. Ah. Forgive my harsh tone." The funny thing was, Sasha really did look contrite. "One does not fight with the king. I am...I must remain here until the killer has been found. So," and here he turned back to March,

"I won't have the opportunity. After that—"

March smiled. "After that."

"I guess you've put together a team," I said. "What do we do first?"

Sasha pulled a folded note out of his jacket pocket. "I found this under the stove in Lauren's home. It was quite near where she fell." He handed it to me. "Perhaps she sought to hide it from her assailant."

I didn't need to unfold the paper to know what it was. I recognized the prescription pad, and when I opened it, I recognized the handwriting.

"Doctor Bel gave this to me. I gave it to Marly. Big question: how did Lauren get it?"

11

"So," **March asked, "If Doctor** Bel gave it to you, and you gave it to Marly, how did it wind up in Lauren's house?" He fished the maraschino cherry out of his bourbon and popped it in his mouth with obvious pleasure. I got temporarily struck blind, so Claudio picked up the conversational slack.

"We know Lauren was interested in what happened to Marly. Didn't she go to see her?" After he spoke, we all had the same thought pretty much simultaneously.

"No," I said. "Absolutely not. I know Marly, she doesn't have it in her. She would never—"

"Nah," Claudio agreed. "I mean, I hope not."

"Do you accuse your friend?" asked Sasha. "Marly," he said, almost to himself. "Tell me about Marly." He smiled.

"Marly is angry with Ruby right now," March said, "but she is a teacher of children, her heart is kind and her spirit is one of light. I should know." I wondered what sort of connection he and Marly shared. His touch had brought her back from not only death, but the possession of whatever took hold of your body when you turn into a vampire. Did it just accept defeat and slink off into the ether? Did it fight back? Did it fight back against Lauren?

"I'm going to go see her," I said. "Tomorrow." Both March and Sasha looked like they wanted to jump in on this trip, so I quickly added, "March, she knows you, so you should come. Sasha, I think you better sit this one out. We can come by Lauren's place after we talk to her."

Sasha regarded me coolly. "Then there is no reason for me to linger." He left by the door rather than dematerializing. I wondered if he could only do that trick to and from the Unseelie court and how he got around town, but then I figured if his king could hook me up with my own driver, they could find something for him, too. I pictured him on one of those electric scooters, and it was quite an image.

Claudio leaned over the bar and whispered, "Is there any scenario that ends with the two of them making out?" I slapped my hand over my mouth to cover my bark of laughter.

"I'd love to know what brings you so much

pleasure." March was watching me curiously.

"You do, of course. Let's get this place cleaned up so we can talk about it." I didn't figure the real reason would go over too well. It wasn't a lie, just a little rearrangement of the facts. I mean, it was technically true.

Claudio and I made quick work of closing up The Hare, and I pretended my new pal James was a random Uber driver. March and I could have that conversation later. He listened carefully to the reggae on the radio and told me he'd decide later if he liked it.

"It sounds like smoke tastes," he said, and I had to admit he was not wrong. In the rearview, I could see James smile.

"I think you'll come around on it," I told March. "Maybe I'll put together a playlist for you." James winked at me, and I covered my own smile with my hand.

Finally, we were back in my place, alone. From the front walk to the bar to that other place—the Field of Significant Conflict—and a short ride up 16th Street, it felt like a lot longer than the maybe two hours since he'd reappeared. He was that way, though. Time did funny things around him, almost like it was trying to get his attention, the way a cat winds between your legs. Whatever was going on in his head, whatever brought him back to me, that much hadn't changed.

I locked the door and tossed my backpack on the

kitchen table. I wasn't completely over my concern (no longer obsession) with keeping vamps out, so the lights were already on. On the other hand, I spent a lot less time worrying that I still smelled like a vampire——like garbage——so my collection of body wash and scented candles took up less space in my house. After what happened last year, with March and Marly and me, I was slowly getting back to normal. Then I looked at March. Maybe normal was overrated. I think I was right, that he carried a sort of glow from place to place. Just jeans and a grey t-shirt that had once been black. I wondered where he got his clothes from, whether some other woman had pulled the thin cotton of his shirt down to cover the downy, golden skin of his stomach (which, if I remembered correctly, seemed a bit flatter than before. Was he on a new workout routine, out there in his woods?) Had other hands buttoned his jeans? Or unbuttoned them? Rather than making me jealous of some imaginary rival, the idea got me going.

"I like that t-shirt," I told him. "I wouldn't have guessed you were a Fugazi fan, though."

"I like bands," he replied. Then he looked concerned. "This is a band, right? Like Firefall?"

"Pretty much exactly the same thing," I said. "So take it off."

"Ah, good," he said, sliding out of not only the faded black t-shirt but his jeans as well. "I was worried you wouldn't want to. Because you were angry."

I let him help me with my clothes. He held my top in one hand, and my pants in the other. He looked around, not knowing what he was supposed to do with them. He set them on top of his clothes, on the floor. That seemed a very March thing of him to do, and I had to laugh. "That's part of being human, I guess." I reached for him. "I can be angry and then get over it, but I wanted to the whole time. Even when I was mad at you." I got over it, for this, for right now. I ran my hands over his chest, his shoulders, that trail of dark golden hair leading to his already rising cock which bumped against my stomach, demanding attention. I kissed his collarbone and throat. I would have devoured him if I could. Then I remembered I could.

"There's something I didn't get to do, the last time we were together. Gonna take care of that right now." I grabbed a couple of beers and headed for the bedroom. When he realized what I had in mind he looked delighted, like it was a party and he was the guest of honor. I knelt between his long legs and caught his expression of simple, expectant happiness, and he was so beautiful I had to look away. Fortunately, I had something else (also quite attractive) to focus on.

I don't know what I expected, but he was salt and sweet, and then only sweet. He nudged the back of my throat and that was fine, and his soft gasps of pleasure set me on fire. It couldn't be a surprise for him, he must have gotten oral in his long, long life—

but he made me feel like I was the first, the best, the most gifted...oh, wait...the March Effect. Eh, I'll take it. When he climaxed, I again was treated to his one weird superpower of seeing through his eyes, but instead of seeing the top of my head, it was a shattered kaleidoscopic explosion of color with blue and purple and tender new green, slowly settling into a shifting, sighing sea.

I sat up and licked my lips.

"How is it possible that you taste like whipped cream?"

He grinned sleepily at me. "I'm a unicorn, Ruby. I can do lots of things."

I laughed. "Of course. Sure. Of course you can. I'm sorry I can't do the same thing."

He sat up, looking offended. "Don't you even think about it. I've been waiting for this exact moment." Then he paused. His eyes became unfocused. "This moment. I'm now. This is now. There are no knives."

"Knives! No, I should hope not. Come back, babe." I kissed him. "Is it hard for you to focus? On now?" I wondered how worried I ought to be.

He shook his head. "No. It's nothing." He was a terrible, no-doubt unpracticed liar. "I'm now," he repeated. "And this is now." He pulled me close and kissed the back of my neck. "And you smell..."

I jerked in his arms. "I smell?"

"Like honey in the sun." I was being stupid. I forced

myself to relax.

He dipped his head. "And you taste just as you did—as you do. Like sweetness and salt," he murmured, and his mouth was unbearably soft. "Like velvet grass two minutes before dawn. Like flowers that only bloom in the rain." I don't know if he could see through my eyes, but the explosion was just as gorgeous and just as powerful.

When I could move my arms, I handed him a beer from the nightstand.

After a long drink, he said, "I want to be inside you, but I think I need a minute."

"A minute?" That was a pretty quick reload. "A whole minute, huh?"

"I'm sorry," he said, and I realized he meant it. Then he added slyly, "Not like your other boyfriends?"

"March, you dope," I darted my hand over and pinched his nipple, he gave a very human yelp. "I don't have any other boyfriends."

"You should have as many as you want," he said, "and everything else you desire." He sat up and pulled me upright with him, settling me onto his lap. A cursory examination told me he'd taken his minute and was ready to go.

"You taste like dessert and make me see colors," I reminded him. "That's hard to beat." He took my foot and put it behind his back. "What are we doing?"

"I want to show you something. A place. Colors."

He continued to arrange our arms and legs until we were eye to eye with my legs wrapped around his waist.

Confession time. While I didn't insist on Missionary with the lights out, this was new ground for me. My repertoire was pretty vanilla before the attack, and then it was over six years of trying to not even think about sex. This was strange—not bad, just strange—and I couldn't force myself to relax. That's always the advice, isn't it? Just relax? I'd wanted him, dreamed of him, longed for him for months, and now that he was here—I don't know. It felt jarring. I pretended we were dancing and I let him lead, but for a couple of minutes I felt super awkward. I didn't know where to look, or where to put my hands.

Finally I said, "Okay, what is happening right now?"

"Let's stop," he said. "We'll stop." He gently set down my foot.

"No," I said. "I don't want to stop. Just let me..." I tried re-wrapping my leg around his back.

"It's like driving," he said, reaching for my ankle and moving it back into position. "I was afraid of the other cars, but you took care of me and you took me to places. Let me take you now, little shiny stone. No harm will come."

I smiled and actually did relax, and nodded. "What do I do?"

He lifted me and set me back down, achingly slowly now that he was buried deep inside me. It felt strange sitting up—he was practically making a U-turn—but he was hitting places inside me I'd only read about, and it was intense. I didn't want slow anymore. "What now?" I gasped.

"Breathe with me," he said. "Follow me."

That sounded like every yoga class I never went back to, but I figured I'd give it a try if only because he seemed really into it, and I liked his driving analogy. So I did. And he did. And then...something shifted. I wasn't feeling self-conscious, I was feeling our hearts beating, our blood rushing...together. I forgot to be worried about what my face was doing. As I fell into his rhythm, my hands found safe purchase. I hung onto his shoulders, and we managed to breathe together and move and kiss all at the same time. I could feel him swelling inside me with each breath, and it felt so sweet and so close.

"You are ready," he said against my ear. "Come with me."

I was mentally prepared for some version of his light show, but as we peaked together, I opened my eyes to find us in another place. Unlike the place I'd accidentally visited earlier, this was lit by an unseen but gentle sun, and I could hear bells chiming somewhere far away. We were...swimming? Floating? In a warm and golden sea, and every heartbeat radiated the colors of the sky and the sea around us. Still joined, still pulsing and still moving together. Our minds had followed the example of our bodies and were mingled together, and for those few moments, I knew what it was like to be him—magical, perfect, a bearer of light. I was weightless. I was free.

12

I floated there, buoyed by the glinting water, and warmed by our shared embrace. *This is what it's like for him all the time,* I thought. *No, how is that possible?*

I wanted to stay, but after a couple more breaths I blinked, and we were back in my bed. We'd kicked the blanket and pillows onto the floor, and pulled half the fitted sheet off the mattress while we were at it. It wasn't an ecstatic paradise, but it was home. At least there was beer.

My head was still swimming and I simply lay with my head on his chest, trying to catch my own breath, waiting for my heart to slow down. I missed the golden ocean right away. My body was limp and sweaty. I felt both lumpy and ungainly, and with our strange connection severed, small and alone. The feeling of dislocation faded quickly, and in a minute or two I was just deliciously limp. No ocean, just a sea of endorphins to soak in.

"Colors," he said, sounding pretty pleased with himself.

"Yeah, colors. What was that?" With some difficulty, I lifted my head. He looked totally relaxed, his hair mussed (still perfect) and had a blissed out smile on his face.

"Not what but where," he said. "I thought you deserved someplace nicer than the Field. That hurt you. This was good for you." Another place. At some point I was going to have to have a conversation with myself about the fact that my boyfriend was not even close to being human, and another chat about how after eight months of not a word, he got to be my boyfriend in the space of three hours. But for now, I just inhaled his pine forest smell and melted against the warmth of his skin. "I know it was a strange sort of place, but I thought you'd like it." He stroked my back and an echo of golden light rippled through me.

"I did," I said. "Very much. But where is it?"

He thought about it for a minute. "Not on a map. Not on your phone. I don't think you could go there without me. Or someone like me. Like, the Field is made of enmity and pain. But this place, it's made of desire and pleasure. It is called the Elation Station."

I snorted a laugh, and covered it with a cough.

"Thank you," I said, "for taking me there." We were quiet for a few minutes. "Oh, tomorrow is my night off. I'll cook you some dinner. Think about what you'd like."

"Ah." He kissed the inside of my wrist, but looked away.

"You'd rather go out? Sure."

"Remember how much you liked that place, the ocean. So, now you won't be angry."

"Angry?" He definitely wasn't making eye contact. What was he getting at? "About the Field thing? I already said it was okay."

"No." he said. "Something else. But you shouldn't be angry about it."

I sat up. "Lay it on me." At this point me brain was so hollowed out he could have said literally anything, and it wouldn't have surprised me. *'I'm turning you into a cat.' 'Oh, a cat that's nice!'*

"I thought you would be at your bar and I am seeing Bel—Doctor Bel for dinner. We are having dinner."

So, not a cat. "You made plans with her?" I ran the timeline. "You got in touch with her before you saw me?"

"I wanted to see you. But I had to see her." He took a breath. "Time."

"It's almost 3:30," I said. "It's late."

"Oh, no. I mean, I'm having trouble with time. I think she can help me. And she said there would be noodles. You know I like noodles."

"Yeah, I guess." I pushed back my hair. "How did you talk to her? Did you get a phone after all?"

"No," he said. "I went there. I saw Shanti, too."

"That bitch didn't warn me!"

"I asked her not to. I wanted to surprise you. So you are not allowed to be mad at her." He paused. "Or me."

I laid back down and made sure to pull him close. "Babe, listen. You can't tell me what I'm allowed to be mad about. You just can't. As it is, I am a little annoyed, but you two have a super long history, and I understand you wanting to see her." I guess he figured he was out of the woods and put his arms around me. "The only thing is, please don't talk about me. Other than to tell her I'm fine. I think there are laws that would probably keep her from asking, but—don't."

He agreed not to, and I agreed to end the discussion at that point. Before I fell asleep, I realized I really was annoyed. Not quite angry, but annoyed. And he didn't want me to be, but I was. *How about that*, I thought. *I've vanquished the March Effect, at least for tonight.*

"I want to ask you a question," he said.

"Whuh?" I was still almost all the way asleep. I squinted at the clock—the ungodly hour of 7 am. I blinked my eyes open and stretched, or tried to, because March was curled over and around me, holding me down. The fact that he had a hand on my throat and it didn't wake me up in a blind panic showed good progress on my part. He was holding my hair up and looking closely at my neck, making sure the cure he'd given me had worked to his satisfaction. The skin, once torn and ruined, was now smooth and as perfect as if nothing with dirty fangs had ever touched me. Of course, he knew that, but he probably also knew that same skin would flare with heat—like the rest of me—under his hand. I kind of thought he'd move from my neck down but he didn't.

I sat up, pulling the blanket over my legs. "What kind of question?"

"Do I look older to you?"

I was not expecting that, and I gave a startled laugh. Then I realized he wasn't joking. "No, honey. I told you, you look exactly the same." Had I told him that?

"You don't. I thought you did but you look eight months older. Here." He touched my forehead. "There's a line there, it wasn't there before. Maybe I have one, too."

"March," I said, "I am twenty-six years old, I do not have wrinkles. And neither do you." My tone softened. "Are you worried about aging? Is that what's wrong?"

He shook his head. "I think I asked the wrong question. I mean, can you see, when you look at me, that time has passed?"

"No. And I won't." This was a deep conversation before coffee, but even so I was beginning to see what he meant. "When I look at you, I can only see you now. I can't see you from last year. I can compare the memory of you, but memory is unreliable. I can only go by what's in front of me."

He watched me closely, trying to follow. "The me from then is gone is what you're saying?"

"Does this have something to do with the time thing? That you want to talk to Dr. Bel about?"

He gave a sort of groan of frustration and pulled his hands through his long hair. It seemed like he was close to knowing how to say it, but not quite there yet. Then he spotted a book on my nightstand—*365 Daily Affirmations*. Claudio got it for me over the holidays, for some reason, he thought I needed it.

"This," March said. "This is me." He sat the book on its spine on the bed so the pages stood up in a fan.

"You're a book?"

"No, this! This." He ruffled the pages. "These are my memories. This is my life. And before, I could stop on any page, any time I wanted to." Again, he looked frustrated. Language was so limiting for him. "It's like the difference between reading the page, and trying to remember what the page said. It's not the same." He let the pages fall open, then held three or four up between his fingers. "And these are you. Every moment of you, all at once."

"And you could keep it straight in your head?" It sounded like the refracted way a fly or bee sees the world, but with experiences instead of images.

He nodded. "And this one is 'now.'" He pointed at the last page. "Here and now with you—a fixed point I can find. But the rest of 'you' are still right here."

"So," I said slowly, "Now with me is like the most recent time with me, but now with someone else is a different now?"

"I guess it sounds more confusing than it felt."

"Yeah, slightly. Okay. So, what's changed?"

He closed the book. "Sometimes I can't tell if I'm living, or re-living. It began not long after I left you. I went home, and it was winter. It snowed. But then," he rubbed his eyes, "it was summer. At first I thought I'd slept the season away. But then—snow again. And then I began to see you, but I knew you couldn't be there..." He gave me a worried look. "And when I would do what you would call magic, it got worse."

"The pages were out of order?"

He looked relieved; I understood him. "Exactly. I couldn't find now. That's when I decided to come back here. I have to be careful to be here, in the now." He reached across me for the empty bottle of beer. "I need to think about this some more." He considered the dark amber glass. "This only exists now, here. Not the building where it was bottled, not in the field where the wheat grew, or the river, or the orchard..."

It sounded frustrating and confusing, but I was sure Dr. Bel could help him sort it out. I took the bottle out of his hand. "Can you join me here in the present?"

The shower wasn't quite the glittering ocean of our dreams, but it certainly had its pleasures.

Once I was on my feet and dressed, I headed for the kitchen. I picked up the can of Bustelo coffee and gave it a shake. Empty. I needed to do a grocery run, do laundry, clean the house, pay my cable bill, apparently make a dentist appointment, and maybe even look at my email. I also really needed to check in with that traitor Shanti, but all I wanted to do was take March's hand and head back to the bedroom. In the end, my caffeine addiction prevailed.

"I need some coffee, like, desperately. Let's go and pick something up and then we can drive over to Marly's place."

"Will she talk to you?" He pulled on the same jeans and shirt he'd shown up in. I wondered where he did laundry, or if he even needed to. His clothes still looked freshly pressed and smelled delicious after spending the night on the floor in the living room. I, on the other hand, would have sooner walked out of the house wrapped in Lauren's pink bathmat than recycle my outfits, particularly when I was covered in bar effluvia. But we pulled ourselves together and walked down the street to the cafe.

"I don't know. But even though she's still pissed at me, I bet she'll talk to you."

I got my usual, a double espresso with a tablespoon of half-and-half. He ordered some god-awful sounding combination of coffee, mocha, macha, vanilla, caramel and extra whipped cream. To no one's surprise, the barista gave me my drink along with the usual dirty look, while March got his with a heaping helping of heart eyes. They even spelled his name right on the cup. (Mine read 'FURBY'.) And they only charged him for a flat white. If I ordered something like that the people on line behind me would have staged a coup, and it would have cost eighteen bucks. The March Effect strikes again.

"Are you sure you don't want some? It's really good." I took a pass, although I have to say it was a pleasure to watch him go to work on that whipped cream. I wondered if that's where he got the idea.

We took my car up to Marly's neighborhood. I figured it was possible March might recognize James from our last ride, and I didn't want him dwelling on how much I owed or didn't owe the Unseelie king. I parked down the street from her apartment building. It wasn't like I wanted to sneak up on her. Well, actually, that's exactly what it was like. I could tell myself whatever I wanted a thousand times, but I knew very well that thinking she should just get over it was self-serving and cowardly. Mostly I wanted us to go back to the way we were, and if that meant a screaming match, March was there to referee.

But first I had to see her. My plan was to blame it on her kids—they insisted I check on her. I had a whole speech planned. I didn't get to use it. Either she wasn't home, or she wasn't answering the buzzer. Her building was three stories, and her place was on the top floor, so I couldn't look in the window, and there wasn't a doorman for me to throw March at.

"What do you want to do?" he asked. I knew if we waited for someone to come along, he could probably talk them into letting us in, but at the moment no one was around. We got back in the car.

"Well," I sighed, "we'd better go see what Sasha is up to." He got a definite look on his face but didn't reply. "After all, it's his investigation." March put on his seat belt, making a production number out of getting it latched. "I know you don't like that thing—"

"But I don't have a choice because of car danger. I understand how it *works*, Ruby."

I had to laugh. "You are being such a bitch. Finish your coffee." As we drove off, I glanced up at Marly's window. It may have been my imagination, but I could swear I saw the curtains move—a flash of orange? As we pulled into traffic, my phone rang. I stopped at a light and looked at the screen. It was Marly.

"Oh my god," I said to her, "I've been losing my mind—"

"Is March in the car with you?" she asked. Her voice sounded thick, like she'd been crying.

"Yeah, he's here. We're both so worried— "

"Put it on speaker."

I did, and handed March the phone so I could drive.

"I don't want..." she said. Then, "Leave me alone. Both of you, and your friends. You have to."

"Marly, if something's wrong— "

"The one thing, you were right about one thing."

"What?" I asked.

"You did smell. You stink, you still do. Everyone knows it."

I gasped. "That's not true."

"Isn't it?"

"Marly, no. Why are you saying this?" I pulled onto a side street and stopped the car. It was hard to see the road.

"You're a selfish bitch, and he's just as bad. He doesn't love you. No one loves you, you smell like dead fish. So, stay out of my life. Is that enough?"

The line went dead. March shut off the phone, "Something is wrong."

"No shit!" I angrily brushed the tears off my face. "I know she's pissed, but..."

He touched my arm. "I'm sorry."

I shook my head. "I fucked her over, she's got every right to be mad. But that was nuts" I drew a deep, shaky breath. "I'm going to pretend she didn't say all that stuff for now. So let's, um, let's think about what else she said. Leave her alone, she was talking about you and me. But 'friends?' Who does she mean?" We both knew who she meant. A friend who wouldn't ever bother her again.

I drummed my fingers on the wheel. "I mean, why would she tell us to make Lauren leave her alone if she was the one who...look, the Marly I know wouldn't dream of hurting anyone. But I didn't think she'd be capable of saying those things, either.

"I feel that something's wrong," he repeated. "So, do you stay away?"

"Hell, no," I struggled to put on a smile. "Gotta give her a chance to apologize, right?" As much as she hurt me, I knew March was right. Bringing her back from being a vampire wasn't the end of what happened to her. It was still happening.

By now, I'd parked near Lauren's building, and I was treated to a stare-down between March and Sasha, who was waiting for us on the corner. Today, he wore a long-sleeved white button-down patterned with microscopic teal dots and contrasting collar and cuffs in the same shade, paired with slim charcoal trousers and some loafers that were definitely Italian, which is just a wild guess speaking as someone who knows nothing about men's footwear. Guy had taste, if nothing else. He was holding a different pair of expensive looking gloves. Dude must really hate the idea of touching anything in our dirty human world, I guess but admittedly that was not the weirdest thing about Sasha. Top ten, probably. I told him a redacted version of what Marly said, and he nodded.

"So, you tried and you failed. Perhaps I will have better luck." He paused. "Where is she?"

"Nah, dude, she won't let you in. She just told me ten minutes ago to make my friends leave her alone, and that includes you." Even if there was a chance she'd talk to him, I wasn't eager to hear more of whatever else she wanted to tell me. "We should go ahead and call the number on the note you found. I guess a receptionist can at least tell us where the office is."

"Fine," he answered, "You may operate the phone."

"Right," I said. "Since it's my phone." He pulled the notepaper from his pocket. I punched the number in.

"You've reached Doctor Michael Kennedy. If this is an emergency dial 9-1-1. If you'd like to reach the main desk, press 1. To leave a message, wait for the beep." I hit 1 and waited. It turned out to be another recording. "You've reached Columbia Heights Urgent Care on 14th Street. If this is an emergency—" I hung up.

"It's an urgent care," I told the two of them. March looked confused and Sasha nodded like he ran a chain of clinics back home. "A place for sick people to get help. And I got the address. It's not too far. I can drive us over there."

"I shall make my own way," said Sasha. "Show me where it is." I held up my phone, and he scowled at the map. Then, with a glance at March, he turned and walked off.

“He can’t get in your car,” March said. “He acts as if he is above indulging in human things, but he can’t touch the iron.”

“He’s allergic to my car?” That explained the gloves. I wondered what else he couldn’t touch, and whether he was more sensitive than Lauren, because I couldn’t recall her ever wearing gloves. She hadn’t ridden in my car either, though. “Well, we’ll just get there first, I guess. That may be for the best.”

“Yes,” March agreed. “For the best. He’s not a people person.”

13

The trip across town was the usual series of March's controlled gasps and white knuckling the door handle through every intersection. At least he waited until I came to a complete stop before jumping out. Walking up to the clinic, I found we had a surprise waiting for us: Sasha had somehow beaten us there. He was holding his gloves and watching the cars and people going by, judging them all. When he saw us approach, he finished pulling the creamy brown leather gloves on.

"Nice," I said, nodding to the gloves.

"Cat skin," he replied.

I managed not to barf. "Uh, cool. Listen, this is where the doctor works. Do you want to talk to the receptionist?" I figured it was a good chance for him to take point, but to my surprise, he didn't leap into action. He got a weird look on his face, and it took me a minute to realize he was no longer glaring at me. He looked nervous.

"May we speak?" His glare snapped back on and he looked at March. "Privately?"

March waved a hand. "Whatever." Before I could stop him, March went into the office. Well, that was great.

I turned back to Sasha. "What?" I might have raised my voice more than I intended.

He took a breath and stared at his leather-clad hands. "I told you, I don't do this part. I mainly confront those who are about to receive justice. I...need your help." He looked at the clinic, at the big windows and the fluorescent lights. "And his, I suppose." He sighed. "I fear those inside would not be eager to help me. And I sense cold iron all around, inside, in the walls. I may not be the right person for this particular job."

"Okay I have an idea. Why don't you go back and get Lauren's notes together? She wrote everything down—on her hand?" I mimed the way Lauren had taken notes on her palm. "There must be records of what she wrote. Right?"

He swallowed. "Yes."

"Well, have you looked at them?"

"I haven't...I really haven't done anything." He looked back up at me, and for once he looked like a person talking to another person. "I mean, I've sorted through them, but so much of it, I don't know what it means. I haven't known where to start. I don't normally—"

"Do this part. Got it. Well, I can help you with the stuff you don't understand," I said. "Hopefully she'll say if someone was threatening her."

He raised a brow. "Whomever that might be. That is the part I am better acquainted with."

"Yeah, whomever." We'd burn that bridge when we got to it. "I'll come over later, I can go through them with you. You won't have to worry about touching weird stuff." We could do it while March and Dr. Bel were having dinner; it would give me something to do other than sit around and think dark thoughts about what my therapist (my ex therapist?) and her ex-boyfriend (my current boyfriend?) were talking about over red wine and pasta.

He nodded slowly. "Perhaps that would be best." And I guess that was good enough for him, because he turned and headed back in the direction of Lauren's neighborhood, now his temporary home. March was right about his people skills.

"Okay, bye," I said to the air, and went inside the clinic.

The air conditioning was cold, and the office was quiet—just a guy who was a little green in the face sitting in one of the uncomfortable looking plastic chairs with his head leaned back against the wall and a young woman sitting with a little girl in a red and white sweater. The kid was playing with her mom's phone and coughing. Other than that, it was empty. Lucky break. I've gone in with a UTI and nearly died of old age waiting to be seen. March was backed into the corner, trying to hide behind two lab coats and a leftover umbrella hanging on hooks.

"Dude," I said quietly, "what's wrong?"

"There are sick people here," he told me.

"I don't think they can hurt you," I said, thinking of Sasha's allergies.

"But I can't help them." He nodded in the direction of the young man. "That one is easy. He had too much drink. All he needs is water and something to eat. His brains are dry, and that's why his head hurts. He'll be fine." He shot a worried glance at the little girl. "Not her. She's got a malady in her lungs."

"You can tell that just from looking at them?"

He gave me a strange look. "You can't?" I shook my head. "It's coming off of them, in waves. The child..." He looked ready to cry.

I rubbed his arm, trying to reassure him. "She's here to see a doctor, I'm sure they can help her." Of course, I didn't know that at all.

"I can help her," he said. "If I was myself, I could fix her." I could see the wheels turning. "I'd just need to be alone with her. Just for a couple of minutes."

"Babe, I don't think that'll happen. And if you

did transform...into your...form...it might scare her." I didn't think that was true, either. If I were a three-year-old and a real unicorn appeared, it would be the single greatest day of my life. True, he was less rainbows and fluff, and more light and power, but if you're a little girl, a unicorn is a unicorn. "We couldn't get her alone, anyway. Her mom would be with her." Then I began to wonder...no. I just didn't see how we could get the kid by herself in a room big enough for a full-sized horse. "I'm sorry."

He nodded, but I don't think he was listening to me. "And if I did change back into myself, I fear I would slip." Yeah, transforming yourself into a unicorn *probably* counts as magic. "But how can I not help her? What do I do?"

I knew what he meant, but we were here for a reason. It was time for me to get him to stop thinking about using his power for his own reasons and start using them for mine. The March Effect wasn't magic, it was simply part of who he was. I didn't feel great about it, but it was all for a good cause in the end. Lauren was dead, and March might find us a clue. If I tried to get info out of the bored-looking receptionist, I'd get nowhere fast. I gripped his hand. "Go over to that lady at the desk and ask if Doctor Kennedy is here. Tell her it's important that you speak to him."

Even as distracted and upset as he was, it was fascinating to watch her reaction. It wasn't just his looks—well, it was partially his looks. I'd seen it before, and it played out again:

The receptionist glanced up as he approached, then stopped with her pen hovering in midair. The phone was ringing but she let it go to voicemail. The stack of paper on her desk would have to wait. She stared up at him, and I could see her forcing herself to listen in case he asked a question. Now she was talking and also blushing. They laughed together at something, and she leaned forward, twirling her hair between her fingers and touching her throat just above the collarbone. She was listening to him again, but this time she was nodding vigorously, and writing something down for him. He leaned further over her desk, telling her something meant to be private. She nodded solemnly, and as he walked away she gave me a glance meant to turn me to ash. Then she went back to staring at his fine ass, not even trying to be subtle. Been there, sister.

March was oblivious, of course. If she'd been dismissive or rude, he might have noticed. On his way back to me, he made a show out of fumbling with and then dropping the card the receptionist had handed him, right in front of the little girl. When she picked it up, he clasped her tiny hand in his own. She looked at him with surprise, and then treated the room to the sunniest, cutest gap-toothed smile in town. He smiled back, and it was almost as beautiful.

I couldn't help but notice; she stopped coughing.

14

"I wanted to," said March. "I almost did." I hurried to keep up with his long strides. I didn't know where he was going. I don't think he did, either.

"You did something, though."

He paused to let me catch up. "I...I don't know how to say it. I calmed her malady. It won't last. But it was all I could do."

"Why didn't you?" He knew what I meant. I could see through the sorrow in his beautiful, forest colored eyes what it would have been like...taking a long moment to reacquaint himself with four slender legs, a new vantage point from nearly seven feet up, maybe kicking or rearing out of the sheer joy of being back in his own skin. And then channeling the power, all that power, through his silvery, shining body, up through the horn. Everyone in the room, everyone passing by the big windows would have felt the rush of energy and seen the radiant light. Inside, close to the unicorn, we'd likely have had to look away, cover our eyes. It would have been over quickly. The little girl would have been cured of not only what apparently was killing her, but everything else, too. No disease would find her, ever. Only old age would be able to touch her, because that isn't a malady, but a part of life. A brilliant flash of light, and March would have—probably with some reluctance—returned to the human body he'd put on so recently. And then what?

He looked away. "I would have revealed myself. Someone is always watching. And then it's never just one. And it's never enough." He raked back his hair. "I am selfish to say so. But it's happened before. I became... drowned? No. Trapped."

"You can't say no." I nodded, thinking of the endless lineup of people begging to be cured.

"I was not given the opportunity to say no. But that was a long time ago." He sighed. "I told Renee that the doctor needs to look at the child's lungs. I told her it was really important. I think at least I gave the child some time of ease. That, I could do."

"So you *can* heal people when you're...like this?"

"No." He thought about it for a minute. "It's more like I can speed things up. Like, if she had a skinned knee, I could speed up her bruise to where it didn't hurt her, and then let the rest of her body catch up. But if I were to speed up whatever's in her lungs..."

I was thinking cancer, growing and spreading. "It would just grow until it killed her."

He nodded. "I eased her pain. That was all I could do." He glanced at me unhappily. "It makes me slip, though. Sometimes."

"But you're okay right now?" He nodded. "Then maybe we got lucky."

"In magic, there is no luck. There is only balance. But I had to try, even so."

"If you slip, I'll pull you back. And if you told Renee it was important, they'll do it." I had to assume Renee was the receptionist. I looked at him more closely, he was still shaken. "Are you okay?"

He shrugged impatiently. "There's nothing wrong with me."

"Fine." He was either being literal-minded and not understanding me, or he didn't want to talk about walking away from a sick kid. I wanted to ask him about the time he got drowned, or trapped—where and when, and how he escaped. But that, at least, could wait. "So, what did she tell you about Doctor Kennedy?"

He looked at me curiously. I think he forgot the reason we were there in the first place. Then he nodded. "Oh. Doctor Mike. That's what she called him. She said...it's funny." He pulled the business card out of his pocket and handed it to me. On the back was an address in Upper Northwest. "She said to tell Doctor Mike that they found his mail."

"His what?"

"Mail. Like, letters. Correspondence. She said they found his mail in the trash. I guess he was looking for it. She said to tell him to check in. He's on vacation." He paused. "She said I was the second person to come in asking about him."

"Oh." Uh oh.

"So we should go see him?"

"This is really bad. Did she describe the first person?" I held my breath, hoping it wasn't a young brown woman with really cool hair who recently started wearing night time sunglasses. But he shook his head.

"I didn't think to ask." He looked at me warily. "Do I need to go back?"

I couldn't force him to, he clearly didn't want to, and maybe it didn't matter. We'd find out, one way or the other. "Let's go visit the doctor."

Doctor Mike lived in a cute garden apartment in Cleveland Park, one of a half-dozen similar yellow brick three story buildings from around the mid-1920s. The street was shady with mature oaks, the crepe myrtles were coming into bloom in front of some of them, and the azaleas were just about finished. Normally, I would stop to do some urban guerilla gardening and deadhead the white rose bush at the front gate, but normally the gate wouldn't be draped with yellow police tape. Normally, we'd have been able to park pretty close, but normally, there weren't six police cars and an EMT truck blocking the street in front of Doctor Mike's building.

"Is it possible," March asked quietly, "that all this is for another person?" We were on the other side of the street, along with a dozen or so neighbors, gawking at the cops and trading theories. Lots of cell phones were out. This was going to be big on #UpperNorthwest Twitter.

"Anything is possible," I answered, although I surely would have been surprised. "Walk slowly and see if we pick up anything."

"Did you hear what happened?" A tiny old lady in a sunhat with a straw flower stuck on it waved her cane at March. "Poor Doctor Mike," she bellowed. She wore a man's white wife-beater layered over a long purple t-shirt along with saggy black leggings and Birkenstocks. She smelled, not unpleasantly, like weed.

"No ma'am," he answered. "I did not." He stopped and waited for what he needed to come to him.

The woman lived across the street, that was her house right there, she and her husband, "He died back in 07, best man who ever lived, liked to take a drink from time to time, now you tell me if that makes someone bad because I don't think so, lived there since 1947, seen this neighborhood change a lot, used to be quiet, now it's all pregnant gals with yoga mats and strollers walking around with their bubbies hanging out like heathens, everyone's got a dog, too, and don't think I don't see who lets their dogs do their business in my yard, it's not all bad though, I think there's even some of those young men living together if you know what I mean, I say live and let live, they sure do take care of their houses, nice yards, too, I hear they're good with flowers, in fact, poor Doctor Mike, there was talk that he was that way, he did have one of those rainbow flags in his window, and I guess that means something, but I never heard him say a cross word, not like some people I could tell you about."

I think she was happy to have someone to talk to. I was starting to be sorry it turned out to be us. I had to notice the wide berth her fellow gawkers gave us. March and I nodded and gave the occasional 'uh-huh' in her direction as she filled us in on her evil neighbor, whose main crime seemed to have been parking in front of the old lady's house, but that long-ago offense had snowballed into a list of grievances that, according to our new friend, might even include the murder of poor, possibly gay Doctor Mike.

"I wouldn't put a thing past her. She may look nice but she's as mean as a snake. Why, one time, it must have been near Christmas—we were allowed to call it Christmas back then—she took her dog—"

Part of me wanted to make a run for it, but I

interrupted. "So, do you know how it happened?"

She blinked at me. "Well, first all those Supreme Court lib'ruls made it the next thing to a crime to call it—"

"I meant what happened to Doctor Mike." The woman looked miffed at having her theory cut off, but she sniffed and said, "Happened couple days ago, and they just now found him. Mail piling up, that's how they knew. Blunt force trauma. I heard they think it was a crowbar to the back of the head. And the place ransacked." She crooked a finger at us to listen closer, and her voice dropped to a low roar. "I hear they were looking for drugs. You know how those people are."

"Shit," I said.

"Language," she said.

"Thank you, ma'am," said March, and we made our escape.

"You come see me anytime," she called after us—after him, really. "I need a ride to the grocery store next Tuesday, you come by and we'll have some lunch after."

March looked at me with panic. "I don't have a car," he said urgently.

"I'll look for you around 9," she yelled.

"You don't have to take her grocery shopping," I told him. That seemed to calm him down. "But I guess you know what this means."

He nodded solemnly. "I can never come to this street again."

I laughed and gave him a hug.

15

Since we had some time before March had to leave for his dinner date, we went to the zoo. It was free (like everything in D.C.—it's either free or you can't afford it), and while I considered taking him to see the pandas, I also wanted to sit and think of reasons why my best friend couldn't possibly be a vicious, cold-blooded killer. I kept coming back to her night time sunglasses. What if only part of her came back as a human, and the other part came back hungry? Hungry, and angry.

The zoo was a good place for working things out. There were lots of places that weren't overrun by kids and tourists, if you didn't mind looking at creatures more pedestrian than those diva-ass black and white bears. Me, I liked to hang out with the sea lions. They never hide, they seem as entertained by humans as we are by them, and there was an actual in-the-shade place to sit. The covered part was cool even on a hot day, and had a drive-in movie screen sized window to watch the underwater shenanigans of the residents. I wondered what reaction, if any, he would get out of the animals, and the sea lions did not disappoint. They dove and circled, dove and circled, shoving each other out of the way trying to get as close to March as they could. He placed his open hand on the glass, and they crowded around like he was a bucket of fish. We sat on the row of benches in the back, and they took up a sort of respectful watch, one following the other to check and see he was still nearby. We were quiet for a few minutes.

"So, a crowbar. That's made out of iron, right?" March leaned back against the wall.

"Yup. Could be the same person. But Lauren's apartment wasn't ransacked." I thought about it for another minute. "The mail. The receptionist said a stack of mail got stolen off his desk, right? I wonder if the killer was trying to get his home address."

March nodded. "Renee wouldn't give that information out to just anybody. She's very responsible."

I tried to picture angry, busted-looking Marly talking to the receptionist. I didn't think she'd get what she wanted. She'd...anyone would have to find out another way. From mailing labels, for instance.

"I don't know what's considered normal around

here," March said. "Are there a lot of murders with pipes?" I didn't answer. "You'd have to get very close. You'd be able to see their eyes. They would try to fight back. It seems like an intimate sort of way to kill someone. I think this is an angry person."

"Or persons," I said, hanging on to my hopes.

"Her hand," said March. "I can't get it off me." I felt him go rigid next to me.

"Who? The old lady?" I turned to look at him, he was sitting bolt upright, his eyes wide. He clutched the bench; his fingers were white.

"There is danger here," he said. "Are we...is there danger?"

I sat up too. "Is there? Do you, uh, sense something?" Or someone? Wearing sunglasses and holding an iron bar?

"Don't touch me!" I could see his pulse racing in the hollow of his throat.

"What's wrong?" He was starting to scare me. The sea lions were swimming faster; dark, lithe shadows wheeling and spinning past the window. "March?"

He looked at me, reached for me, and pushed my hair away from my neck, looking at where my scars used to be. "It's gone...but I thought I was the one... When did I...?'

Splashing, barking and splashing. The sea lions were lined up along the top edge of the window, slapping the water and barking like angry dogs. I got to my feet and took hold of his shoulders.

"What's wrong?" I shook him a little, but I don't think he noticed. Behind us, water sloshed over the top of the tank. The sea lions were howling, throwing themselves against the glass. I had to get him out of there. Of course, we were directly across from the wolves, and would also have to pass the elephants and god knows what else. This had been a terrible idea.

He looked up, terrified. I don't think he was seeing me. " Knives... there are blades...knives...her hand, her hand upon me..."

A blade...a saw? Did he think we were back on Kenyon Street, facing Margaret and the men with the hacksaw? I knew he was in trouble, but this was beyond trouble. All I could do was hope I could bring him back. "Look at me." I stood over him, blocking him from the animals' view with my body as much as I could. "March, look at me. The men with the saw are gone. Margaret is gone. They can't hurt you. It happened last year. We're safe."

"Knives," he said, but with less panic in his voice. Then he closed his eyes and the tension went out of him. This was his payment for helping that little girl. This was him slipping. I hated magic.

I stroked his silky hair back from his face. "Are you with me?"

After a long, shuddering breath, he was. He blinked a few times, and frowned. "What's wrong with the sea lions?"

I looked over my shoulder. They had quit barking and were coming down from their freak out, still swimming in acrobatic circles, still watching us. A zookeeper, a young woman in khaki shorts with a dark brown ponytail under a FONZ ball cap, came racing around the corner.

"What happened?" she asked. "Did you see it?"

I stepped forward. "They got all upset a few minutes ago. I think a kid threw something in the tank from the other side, but I couldn't really see."

She rolled her eyes. "Terrific. Friggin' kids. Every time. Well, let me go take a look." She went to the window, and the sea lions, recognizing their friend, nuzzled the glass. "What's up, guys?" Once she was certain the animals were relatively calmed down, she looked back. "I guess they're okay now..." They were back to their endless, graceful, but fortunately no longer frantic loops, diving down to check on March, and then get bumped by the next in line. The woman narrowed her eyes at us. "Don't, like, tap on the glass or anything. They don't like that."

"We were just leaving," I said. "I hope your sea lions are okay." I took March by the arm and hauled him to his feet, and he followed me away from the giant tank. As we passed the enclosures on our way back to the exit, howls, grunts and shrieks followed after us. Next time we'd go to the museum.

We didn't talk much on the ride back to my house. He ignored the passing cars and stared straight ahead. Even when I almost got cut off by a scooter, he didn't look up, and that was usually good for at least a hand slapped on the dashboard.

He followed me inside, and sank onto the couch. I got us both beers, and sat next to him. "How bad is this?"

He rubbed his face with his palms. "I don't know."

"You said you were slipping. Is this what you meant when you told me the pages got mixed up? You'll wind up reliving something that already happened?"

"Already, hasn't yet—I can't tell. I'm afraid that I'll pick the wrong page too many times, and then I won't be in the now anymore. Sometimes the path is straight. Sometimes I can see clearly and find the 'now.' Or it only lasts a few seconds. But then..." he closed his eyes. "Everything is at once, and I can't tell if it's real." I put my arm around his shoulder and he leaned against me. "And you're there, in every time. You, and knives. That's why I came back. To protect you from the knives. I'm sorry. I should have told you sooner."

"Don't apologize to me, save it for the sea lions." No wonder he was so freaked out. It sounded horrible and exhausting, like not being sure if you were dreaming. I hated that shit. I was well aware I was totally unqualified to give him any useful advice, so I turned to my default:

making a list. It's better than wringing your hands, right? "So let's figure this out. You're having visions or memories. And you can't tell if they're real or not, and they're mostly about me, and about knives. Is that it?"

He was quiet for a minute. I could feel the slow rise and fall of his breath. Then he sat up. "That...I think that's right. It's growing harder and harder to tell when I am." I could see how hard it was for him to put words to whatever was happening to him.

"You said this started when you were mortal for a week? Could it be you're having a bad reaction to once being human?" If we could talk it out, name it, maybe it wouldn't be so bad.

"I think I'm having a bad reaction to not being completely anything. I'm not mortal. But I'm no longer the creature I was. When I spent time as not only human-shaped but actually mortal, part of me changed. I took a life, and then I offered myself as sacrifice. I thought that would balance the scales, but something must have gone wrong. When I was restored to my own form, whatever changed didn't change back. I'm something between. And I don't know if something between is meant to exist."

"March." I touched his cheek. "Why did you come back here? It wasn't just to protect me."

He took my hand. "I have feelings. New feelings. Some of them are about you, some of them I can't name. But I know what one of them is. It's something I've seen in the eyes of mortals many times."

"Tell me," I said.

"I'm afraid."

He hadn't been afraid when Baba Yaga plunged a knife into his chest. The poachers who nearly sawed off his horn hadn't scared him—he'd fought back. But he was afraid now of an enemy he couldn't see, fighting a battle with no rules. "What are you afraid of?"

He wiped tears off my face. "I cannot die, at least." He didn't sound completely sure. "My body—this human body—will still be here. But my mind won't be in it." His look darkened. "And I think that might be worse."

I was out of bullet points. So I put my arms around him again, and we held each other close as my living room went from afternoon into dim evening. It was time for him to leave for dinner.

"Forget what I said about not mentioning me. This is more important. Tell Doctor Bel everything you told me."

"If she can't help me..."

"Let's let her try." I had to hang onto the idea that someone could do something. "Do you want me to go with you?"

He sat up. "I'm okay now. I can see...I'm okay. And she said she was sending a car. I hope she also sends someone to drive it. Why do you smile?"

"It's nothing. I'm sure you'll get to her no problem.

And..." I sighed. "Tell her I'll call her tomorrow." In addition to March's time problems, Dr. Bel might have heard from Dr. Mike—she said they were acquaintances. And she might even be able to shed some light on what the deal was with Sasha and his pal the king.

The way I'd avoided her seemed like a lot of childishness. Xeno trauma was literally her job—whether the xeno caused it or experienced it. She'd helped March before, she'd helped both of us. She could help him now. She had to.

16

Once I got March into his car (which came equipped with a driver, we were both happy to see) I grabbed my backpack and headed out into the soft light of early evening towards the place where everyone in D.C. ends up eventually; Mega Slice, home of the world's biggest, greasiest, and most alcohol absorbing pizza. Pushing past the pre-gamers at the counter, I got a plain cheese the size of a manhole cover. It was also pretty cheap, as I didn't want to bust the budget when it was entirely likely Sasha would turn his pointy beak up at me. With our stupid-sized dinner in hand, I stepped onto the curb, phone balanced on the box, ready to call a Lyft. As I did, James pulled up in the Rav 4.

"How did you do that?" I asked him.

He smiled at me in the rearview. "I only have one

job, for the moment. Where can I take you?"

I told him I was heading to Lauren's place, and he merged into the heavy traffic on 18th Street. I noticed he didn't have the typical Christmas tree shaped air freshener hanging from the rear view—he had the same silver medallion I'd seen Sasha wearing; the tree, clouds, the dragon. The sign of the Unseelie king. I figured I'd better try and stop worrying about March before I got to Sasha—he was no fan of unicorns in general and my unicorn specifically, and I didn't want to get into it with him. Time to distract myself with small talk. "You work for him, the king. What's he like?"

His smile faded. "He is fair to me. I do my job and I don't get called before him. Soon, I hope, my job will be over and I'll be free."

"You're...working off a debt?"

His smile returned, but I thought it looked a little forced. "Something like that." His eyes darted from the road to me and back. I could see the hesitation on his face. Finally, he said, "Assume he'll know everything that happens."

"The Unseelie king? I figured Sasha would report back." I leaned forward. "Is this about the king or Sasha?"

"You better than most should know not to close an eye around xenos."

I didn't know how much he knew about me, or if that remark meant he himself wasn't a xeno—I'd assumed he was. “Thanks for the warning.” I settled back into the seat, thinking again of how many xenos I’d let into my life, and my heart. Was he wrong, though? “Is there anything else I should know about the king—?”

“The king of the Unseelie Court is fair and generous,” he said, rather loudly. “Enjoy your evening with the sworn justice of the king, who is duty bound to carry out his will!”

I’m no genius but I can read a room, even when it’s the inside of a car. “Thank you,” I replied in the same stagey voice. “We will certainly work together and... uh...solve the case?” I saw gratitude in his eyes. Someone was listening. Or maybe he was just being paranoid. Or both. “I guess when I’m ready to go home—”

“I’ll be there, not to worry.” His cheer had returned like nothing had happened. “See you after dinner.”

The door troll greeted me like an old friend, which I admit I liked—it felt like an achievement. I took the elevator to *thistle,* keeping an eye out for veil-wearing dental assistants. I guess she was still at work. I did get the stink eye from some sort of wood nymph. She was absolutely gorgeous despite the twigs in her hair and tree-frog eyes. You wouldn’t think someone half a foot shorter than you could look down her nose but this girl was a pro.

“Shouldn’t you be, like, on a bus or something?” Maybe that was the most mortal thing she could come up with. I would have gone with McDonalds, but +10 for effort.

"Shouldn't you be up a tree?" She 'hmphed!' at me like fucking Tinkerbell on the rag and stomped off on her tiny, perfect feet, disappearing around a corner.

Sasha let me in, casting a dubious look at the pizza box. He had on what appeared to be grey cashmere sweat pants and a plain white t-shirt. I could see the outline of his medallion under the fabric. He'd only been here for a couple of days, but I couldn't help but notice his hair, which was damp from the shower, was starting to go grey at the temples. Could your hair be affected by allergies? He also wore some super bougie indoor slippers. I got the impression he took a look at a Calvin Klein ad and went from there. He looked sleek and elegant, and frankly kind of weird plopped down in Lauren's pink and white fluff-palace. I wondered how he lived at home, and if he'd be here long enough to redecorate. Anyway, he did have Peronis in the fridge. I took a second to marvel at the plastic bottle caps. Third floor, guaranteed iron free.

I brought him up to speed on what we found at Dr. Mike's house: a bashed in skull, a body several days old, the place ransacked. I did my best to describe the old lady, our best witness. I left out the sea lions and the fact that March was on a date. Well, a 'date.' And that, despite what he said, he was afraid he was losing his mind. Or dying. Or both.

"And they just happened to find him today. Interesting. Does a doctor often keep drugs at his home?" Sasha asked.

"I don't know. I really don't know any medical doctors. But I guess it's possible."

"So the old human may have been correct about roaming gangs of murderous, iron bar wielding thugs. These two events may in fact be unrelated. As we say at my court, correlation does not imply causation."

"I did not know that." I mean, I knew that expression, I just didn't know it was so widespread. I also didn't know if he was serious or trying to be nice, but I appreciated not having to defend my maybe-vampiric, maybe-killer, maybe-friend. I pushed the pizza box to the middle of the coffee table. "We should eat this while it's still hot."

"What is it?" he asked, cautiously lifting a corner of the lid.

"This is the pizza that made Adams Morgan famous. Usually you have to be on day three of a week-long bender to really appreciate it, but here we are." I took down plates from Lauren's cabinet, stepping carefully around where her body had fallen, although of course by now there was nothing but a clean floor. The gouges left by Shanti's claws had also been repaired. I wondered if Lauren had paid a security deposit, and who would get it back now. I wrangled a piece from the box onto Sasha's plate and put it in front of him. He folded his arms and raised an eyebrow. "It's like bread," I told him. "You know bread, right?" He nodded. "Well, it's based on that."

I dove in, being not only pretty hungry, but also maybe giving him a chance to see how to cantilever a big oily drippy slice into biting position. He watched, not even trying to hide his disdain, and went to get a knife and fork (bamboo, I think) from the kitchen. He then made a performance of cutting a piece and arranging the strings of cheese carefully across the top, took a breath and ate. "This is acceptable," he announced.

"So, what do you guys over in Unseelieland eat for dinner?" I was just trying to make conversation, and it took my mind off of worrying about March. I should have been paying better attention to the dude in front of me. He might have been wearing athleisure, but there was a warrior inside those yoga pants, and now he looked pissed.

"You may call my home the Place of Good Grace, The Seat of Light, the Fair Home, the Elemental Throne, or That Which From all Blessings Flow. Whatever you call it, you will speak of it with reverence, even if it's nothing more than a joke to you. I can assure you, it isn't one to me."

I had been told. "I'm sorry," I said. "I wasn't thinking. I've had a lot on my mind, even though that's a shitty excuse. You're right, I was rude. What would you like me to call it?"

"You may simply refer to it as my court, since proper language obviously eludes you."

Told and burned. This was going to be a long evening. "Ooookay. So, what do you eat at home in your court, then?"

He gave me a hard look. "Are you really interested? Or are you trying to make me over into something more like yourself? Do you think if our people have similar ways of sitting down to meals, we'll forge some sort of bond? Or perhaps you are serious. If you really want to know, of course, I'll tell you. So which is it, mortal girl?"

I swallowed hard. He was right—I was looking for common ground. I wasn't sure how it got turned into an insult, but it was precisely what I'd been doing. I shook my head and forced back embarrassed tears. I wanted to tell him he was a snotty bitch and I was just trying help, but instead I stammered, "Never mind," and finished my slice in silence. So did he.

I took our plates and dumped them in the sink, put the box of leftover pizza in the fridge, and sat back down on the couch. He was watching me. I examined my sneakers.

"I fear I have mistaken ignorance for rudeness," he said. I looked up, surprised. "I think perhaps you meant no harm." He sighed. "Since I am far from my home, I feel its loss quite keenly."

He was homesick, and I was careless. And possibly ignorant.

"Once, we had a really bad president," I said. "You know what that is? Anyway, I was in Europe on a school trip, and even though I hated the guy, I also hated hearing the local people shit on my homeland. So, I get you, and I am sorry."

He nodded. After a moment he said, "We are quite fond of fowl—wrens, pigeons, larks—that sort of thing. And floral garnish. Sauces, aromatics. And sweets, of course. The king has some remarkable chefs in his employ."

I relaxed for the first time in an hour. "Have you ever had tandoori fried quail?" An Indian restaurant near me made one that could make you weep. "I think you'd like it." I made a mental note to get some decent takeout if we did this again. Or maybe just go there. I could see Sasha in a nice restaurant much more easily than I could picture March with a white napkin on his lap, although I had no doubt everyone from the head chef to the busboy would be elbowing each other out of the way to serve him. Hell, take 'em both and see what happens. I took a minute to wonder how March's date with Dr. Bel was going, and how many tiramisus he was going to put away. I didn't wonder if she was going to be able to help him, because I was too busy working on convincing myself she could.

"Perhaps we should look at Lauren's notes?" Sasha said. He reached into the bookcase and took down a folder of thin, almost transparent paper covered in faintly glowing script.

"Is that it?" It was a pretty thick folder. "Well, let's get started." That's when the coffee table reared up on its 'hind' legs and made a mad gallop around the room. Our beers and papers went flying and my bag flew into the wall. We jumped up and wrestled the table back into place, and I grabbed some paper towels to mop up the spill. After a couple of indignant bucks, the table settled down.

"I'm sorry—again. That was me. It's been happening on and off for about a month, and I don't—"

"He's thinking of you. Hopefully he'll be distracted soon—his kind are easily distracted—and it will pass."

I stared at Sasha. "He? He who?"

I got the look I was getting used to from him: utter disdain. "Whom do you think?"

"Are you telling me March is the reason shit's been flying around?"

Now he looked amused. "You didn't know? Hmm, perhaps you two should talk about it. Ask him why he's flinging the furniture." He rearranged the papers on the coffee table. "Seems a petty use of power, if you ask me." He lifted his hands and the papers—and the table—stayed put. "See? It's passed. He's moved on to something else."

I narrowed my eyes. "How do I know you're not making this up because you don't like him?"

He laughed right at me. "I thought you and your

unicorn were so close. And he forgot to mention this?" You could practically smell the contempt in his voice. Honesty would never win Sasha a popularity contest, but it did make him hard to argue with. I gritted my teeth.

"Okay, I got a great idea. Let's go over Lauren's notes, and stick with the reason we're here. How does that sound?"

He shrugged smugly, if that was possible. "I believe that was my idea, actually." Then I guess he couldn't resist. "Make sure to take good hold of your pen, should he chance to think of you again."

And then it was my turn. "Okay, I get it. You think he's terrible. I know why he challenged you, by the way—he told me about your king being after him. See, we do talk about things. So what's your excuse? Why are you so down on him?"

"Really? You can't guess?"

I couldn't. March was a charisma magnet, drawing everyone towards his light. Sasha was more like a walking Nine Inch Nails video—dark and difficult, but compelling. They were evenly matched on the Field of Dumbass Names, too. So what was up his ass?

Sasha glared at me. "He's free. He's got a kind of freedom you and I will never experience, and can only slightly even comprehend. This may be the common ground you were looking for earlier, now that I think of it. He's completely free, and what does he do? Nothing.

He creates nothing, builds nothing, he leaves no trace of himself anywhere. He might as well not exist at all." His mouth twisted. "And you all fall at his feet. Hooves. Whatever."

So Sasha was jealous. But he was wrong. "You don't know the first thing about him. What he is. He changed my life. He literally saved Marly's life. He may not write books or...or...hand out the king's justice, but he's made a mark on the world. Just a different kind of mark."

He gave me a long, contemplative look. "Shall we?" I stared at him blankly. "Look at the notes?"

"Oh. Let's."

In the end, the parts that turned out to be eye-opening were mostly about humans: how much she was learning, how confusing they were, and how much she liked them. Well, me.

I am starting to see why the unicorn was so attached to my human subject. Ruby denies she is in any way out of the ordinary, and if this is indeed true, I am more convinced than ever that our folk should consider more wide-ranging contact. I hope my proposal to extend my stay is ultimately approved. This world has much to teach us.

She had more to say about March.

I am reminded of the old story of Aello. While the principle players are different, there are also some striking similarities. Based on what happened to her, I wonder if March will come back. And if he does (which I believe is quite likely,) what that will mean for Ruby? Again, thinking of the story, I admit I'm glad I'll be here for her.

I guess job one was going to be finding out who/what Aello was, and what it had to do with March, and with me. Lauren seemed to think I'd need a friend, and she was right about that. It was the first thing we had that seemed like a lead.

"Do you know what she's talking about here?" I asked.

Sasha shrugged. "It appears she spent a great deal more time in the library than I did." He turned the fragile page. "Oh look, this one's about you."

'*...Ruby's job is basically that of a servant. Anyone regardless of rank may demand she wait upon their whim. Yes, they exchange goods for services (our most ancient records reveal we did the same—lending further credence to the theory of our being ancestral cousins), but the goods—moneys—have no intrinsic value. Unlike ours, they only seem to be a metaphor for some greater, hidden power. Yet she works herself to exhaustion to acquire them. It appears to be at once the one piece of her life which brings her the least happiness, and that takes most of her time.*'

Looking at her pages of notes, her musings on human life, her affection—and worry—for me, her plans for the future, I felt horribly guilty at how I'd underestimated her. I thought she was a bit of an airhead, even childish. Sweet, sure, but a scholar? I just never knew.

"We have to find out who killed her," I said to

Sasha. "And take them apart."

He smiled. It wasn't a nice smile. "I'm glad you're seeing things my way."

17

After a couple of hours of reading Lauren's neat but tiny print, my eyeballs were ready to fall out. So far, it was just a catalogue of her experiences among the mortals. If anyone had been harassing or threatening her, we hadn't found any record of it yet.

I stood and stretched, and Sasha handed me my backpack. "Thank you for the Mega Slice," he said. He held the door open for me. "It was...thoughtful of you."

"Yeah," I told him, "it happens from time to time. You just have to catch me on a non-ignorant day."

He raised a brow. "Is this bonding? Is that what we're doing?"

"Maybe intro-to-bonding. When we start braiding each other's hair, you'll know we've made it." He took a horrified step back, putting a protective hand over the back of his head. “That was a joke, dude.” I paused. “How do the people of your court say good night?”

“We usually say, ‘Good night.’”

I shook my head and headed for the elevator. What a dork.

I banged the door open, calling out, “March? How did it go? What did Doctor Bel...”

My voice trailed off as I realized I was alone. They were still out. “Fine,” I told myself. “Nothing to worry about.” I took off my shoes and my bra, put on a stretched-out t-shirt, hit the fridge, and draped myself across the couch. “Hello, old friend,” I said to the ice cream. “It’s you, me, and *International House Hunters*, reunited.” I flipped on the TV. “Australia again. Ugh.” I only had a couple bites of chocolate brownie chunk when my phone rang.

“Ruby? Can you talk?”

“Doctor Bel? Is March all right?”

“He’s fine. He’s fine. That’s why I called.”

There was a short pause, it sounded like she was talking to someone with her hand over the speaker. “Is it too late for you to meet me? I’m at Annabelle.”

“You took March to Annabelle?” The bar at the Dupont Circle hotel was super fancy, he’d certainly be the only one in a Fugazi shirt.

“No,” she said, and I could hear a smile in her voice. “But I’m here now. We had dinner down the street. I just sent him home. He has your keys, right?" I said he did. "I feel like we should talk. Now."

This has to be positive, I told myself. *It's something I can do right now. It's going to be good news.* I told her I could meet her there in half an hour, kissed the ice cream goodbye and put my bra back on. To my surprise James wasn't waiting outside, so I ended up jumping on the 42. (My favorite bus. Busses are the future, people.) I guess he was only on-call for Unseelie work events.

I hopped off at N Street and walked a block up to the hotel, where a troll was not there to greet me, just a couple of doormen trying to get a bunch of drunk Hill staffers sorted into cabs. The lobby was typical 'Fancy Washington', all marble columns, white people, velvet banquettes, lots of giant floral arrangements. The bar, Annabelle, was tucked off in a corner of the lobby. You kind of had to know it was there. I hoped Dr. Bel was planning on paying because the martinis ran around twenty bucks. (I mean, they were good, but still.)

It was early in the week and since it was nearly 10 p.m., the place was pretty quiet. It was mainly a bar for the old rich people (hence the prices), with the crowd getting progressively smaller after Happy Hour. Dr. Bel was sitting in a booth in the back and waved me over.

"Wow, you look great," I said. She literally looked at least ten years younger. With her sleek blonde updo and glasses, she'd gone from classy older lady to sexy librarian. I remembered how she told me she could alter her appearance, unlike her younger-but-rancid-looking sister, Baba Yaga.

She smiled. "Thank you. I felt like I was ready to shake things up a bit. How are you?" When she said it, I knew she wasn't making small talk. She expected an answer.

"Honestly, things have gotten really freaking weird. And that was before March showed up." I gave her a searching look. "You said he's okay?"

I was hoping she'd say yes right away, but she paused, thinking. Then she flagged down a waiter. "Another two of these, please." I guessed I was going to have a dry vodka martini with three bleu cheese stuffed olives, then. "March is fine for now, and we will definitely talk about that. But before we do, I want to say something." I waited. She gathered herself, looked up at me and said, "I'm not your therapist anymore."

"You're breaking up with me?" I hadn't seen this coming.

"No, the opposite, sort of." She took a breath. "You didn't really need my help even before we, er, came to a decision about Marly. And after, well. I became something that brought you more stress, not less."

I nodded. "I know I was kind of a dipshit about the whole thing. I blamed you. That was stupid."

"It was what you needed to do at the time. Before I completely let you go, how do you feel now?"

"That you gave me good advice, you did nothing

but help me, and I have to figure out what to do next."

She looked relieved. "Then I declare you fixed." She smiled. "If you ever need to talk, of course my door is always open. But at this point, I think we could both use a friend." She waited for the waiter to set down our drinks. "So, to friends." She had always been big on the importance of a good social circle, and she knew I had a couple of friends missing from my life. Even if she was my pity friend, I'd take it.

"To friends." We toasted and I took a sip. It tasted like fresh icy mountain water with a faint hint of brine. "These are good."

"That's why I come here." She set her glass down. "I hear you talked to Marly." So, she was going to make me wait on March. If he was in trouble—right now, immediate trouble—she wouldn't have done that. I relaxed by a fraction.

"Mostly it was her talking. She said...she had some not nice things to say."

"March told me what happened. He thinks it's more than her anger. He thinks there's something else going on."

Marly had said exactly the right things if she wanted to go in for the kill. I worked on not crying in the bar and told myself that her being insane or possessed was better than her hating me enough to say those things.

I took a shaky breath and said, "The main thing she wanted was for me to leave her alone. Oh, I think she went to that doctor for a blood test." Then it hit me. "Oh my God, did you hear about Doctor Mike?"

She nodded. "That's why I called you. Well, one of the reasons." We both knew what the other reason was. "This fight has crossed the border from xeno to human lives. Generally, battles are fought among one race or the other. This is unusual. And you have a habit of finding yourself in the mix." She took a longer drink. "I only knew Michael a little. Met him at a conference."

"I was wondering if he was like you."

"No." She smoothed a strand of hair behind her ear. "It was a while ago, when we met. He was dating a friend of mine—Matheiu, a djinn, so he knew about us. No, he was a mortal who wanted to help." She looked at me for a moment. "So, he was more like you."

"Well, I'm sorry about what happened to him. So... you said this fight. I guess you're including Lauren." She nodded. "She was..." I found my throat tightening. "I liked her, you know? She was a nice person. And she had a lot going on I never knew about until after she got killed." I used the napkin to blot my eyes. Crying in the bar, after all. "Tell me the truth. Because you're my friend. Did I get these two people killed?"

I wish I could say she leapt to say no, but once again, she looked pensive. "I don't know the why of either one. I can suspect that Lauren learned something from Michael, or that Michael was killed to prevent him from telling her something, or that they had nothing to do with each other at all." She put her hand over mine. "But based on everything from last year, I wanted to tell you in person to be careful. Now, March says the king assigned you a driver?"

"How did he know? I never told him that."

She smiled. "He noticed the king's medallion in the car. He's quite proud of noticing things belonging to humans. My point is, use the car. Stay in touch with me, or Shanti, or March. Or your friend Sasha, I suppose." She frowned. "What do you make of him?"

"He's...strange. Even on a sliding scale not including mortals, he's odd. He doesn't like it here. He's very allergic to iron, so he can't touch a lot of things. He's super devoted to the king over there, but I get the impression the king doesn't feel the same way. His being here—I think he'd deny it, but it seems like he's being punished."

"Hmm." Dr. Bel stabbed an olive with the long cocktail skewer. Each one was shiny black and had a tiny but detailed plastic feather for a handle. "I wonder if a grand gesture might place Sasha back in the king's favor. Rather like the arsonist fireman."

"Whoa." My eyes got big. "You think he's the killer?"

"Do you know for a fact he didn't murder Lauren?"

"Well, yeah. He only showed up after...actually, I found her body and he was already there. He could...I guess he could have killed her and then waited to see who would show up."

"But you don't think that's what happened."

I thought about it. "Honestly, no. He seems...moral? That's not the right word. Honorable. Maybe that's it. Oh," I made my point with my own skewer, suddenly realizing the feathers were supposed to be quill pens. "And he can't lie."

She shrugged. "There's lying, and there's lying. But I trust your senses." She sipped her drink. "March is a little jealous of him, I think."

I laughed. He and Sasha were truly a matched set. "Did he say why?"

She smiled. "March called him a fancy man."

I snorted a laugh so loud the bartender and the waiter looked up at us. I cleared my throat. "You are kidding me."

"That's what he said: 'That fancy man's got Ruby running all over town.' But it's more than that. Based on what I know of the Unseelie fae, Sasha controls serious power. He may seem strange, but don't underestimate him. He is made for battle. And he has purpose. Of course, he's got almost nothing *but* purpose. But that's a thing March never had."

I thought about what Sasha said, how he resented March's freedom. "What's it called when you have so little in common you're practically the same?"

She smiled wryly. "A rom-com with a body count." She ate her final olive. "I admit I was surprised when

March showed up at the office. Shanti was halfway to texting you, but he asked her not to. He wanted to surprise you. I think the concept of 'surprise' is also sort of new to him." She paused "He's got a lot of new things in his head. His past and his present are mixing together, it seems. And time. That's his problem. Time."

I swallowed. "He's coming unstuck, isn't he? He's scared it's going to be permanent." I thought of the fear in his eyes, and my throat went tight. "I think he might be dying."

She got that I'm-a-goddess look in her eye. "I swear to you, I'll do everything I can to help him. And I don't honestly know if he can die."

I shook my head. "He said that, too. But he's changed. Maybe he's changed into something that dies. We've got to stop it."

She contemplated her glass. I think she wasn't used to not having all the answers. "I don't even know for sure what 'it' is. But until we figure it out, I worked a charm for him. Kind of like the mantra I gave you, remember?"

Of course I did. My actual xeno attack was followed by months, and even years, of panic attacks: when I smelled something that reminded me of the garbage stink of a vamp, when someone got too close to me, for no reason at all. And I would say to myself, *I am alive, I am in my body, I have control*. Over and over. Even if I didn't believe it, it seemed to do something to my brain and the sheer pants-wetting terror would slowly evaporate. Between that and a lot of therapy (and Xanax), I called myself recovered. "How does it work?"

She started to speak, then paused. "Consider time as a river. His river seems to be dammed or diverted somehow. I've helped him dig a narrow, fragile channel to help it flow. Like your mantra, it's really just a crutch until we find a permanent solution. So as long as he doesn't use his xeno abilities, he should be stable."

"No magic."

It seemed like a doable stopgap, although I'm sure he wasn't happy about it. Then I remembered the coffee table. "Did it happen during dinner? Did he slip?"

She nodded. "Briefly. He thought he was in a moonlit glade. I think it may be one we visited together. It only lasted a moment. I think he was embarrassed, he was definitely upset. But it was enough that he agreed. No magic." Dr. Bel snagged my remaining olive. "We talked about some other things. Why he came here, for instance."

I thought about what he told me. About new feelings. And fear. "What did he say?"

"He told me you were upset that he made plans with me, that he came to me first. He said he told you not to be, and yet, to his amazement, you were anyway." She smiled indulgently. "This is good for him, I think. First off, you should know I'm seeing someone, so even if he wanted to renew our...relationship—which he doesn't—it wouldn't happen." That explained her glam new look, I guess.

I smiled. "Honestly, I was maybe ten percent annoyed when he told me, but now I'm one hundred percent grateful that he talked to you."

"Well, good. Because the thing is, he came here because of you." I knew that, he'd said it himself, but my brain kept whispering *not that way, not the way you want him to feel.* Hearing it still made my heart race. "He thinks you're in some sort of danger."

He just wants to protect you, my brain said. *See? That's all it could ever be.* "I was hoping that wasn't the only reason."

"Well, he didn't want to tell you at first, because he can't tell when 'it' happens—whatever it is. He says it may even have happened already. He just doesn't know. He said he felt like he was being pulled along by the current—in our time river—and you were the only thing he could hang onto."

"I'm like a temporal life raft that maybe has a hole in it?"

"I'm sure it's more than that. Ruby. He may have feelings for you he doesn't know the name of. He's different. Whatever he's going through now, it started last year when he was mortal, when he was with you. So, you're part of it." She wasn't smiling anymore, just looking at me speculatively. "What is he now? Something that can die? Something that can love? You've changed the changeless. What does that make you?"

I shifted uncomfortably on the slick leather seat. "There's nothing special about me. I just did what anyone would have done. Maybe he would have gotten attached to someone else if they happened to be there that night."

Now I thought she looked slightly annoyed. "He's not a duckling." Then she sighed. "I told you once before to be careful of him. Well, I'm changing that. Be careful with him. His feelings for you—whatever they are—are new to him."

"They're kind of new to me, too," I admitted. It was so, so tempting to name what I felt, and even more tempting to think March felt it too. But that little voice, that reminder that things were always going to be mainly bad, kept reminding me of the March Effect. I could never be sure what I felt was real. And March was probably just grateful he had someone to take care of him while—-

"Oh jeez, I totally forgot. I have to ask you something." I pulled out my phone and showed her the picture I'd taken of Lauren's notes. "Do you know who this is?"

She frowned, reading. "This is an old name. There was a story...." She shook her head. "I'm afraid I'm thin on my Greeks. Sorry."

"Lauren seemed to think whatever happened to this woman has something to do with March. I guess I could google it..."

"Or you could ask Shanti. I'm sure she would know." I looked at Dr. Bel, confused. "Aello was a harpy."

I leaned back in my seat. "I'll call her in the morning. At least she's still taking my calls."

"Of course she is. You have friends, Ruby." She saw my look. "You're thinking about Marly. It may just take some time."

"Or March could be right, and there's something else going on. Something worse. I keep thinking she's the key to all this, but I'm damned if I know how."

Dr. Bel nodded. After a moment she said, "Have you ever heard that drowning people are difficult to rescue?"

That rang a bell. "They fight or something, right?"

"That's right. In their panic and fear, they will fight against the person trying to help them. Sometimes they'll even kill them by pulling their rescuer under. That doesn't mean they should be left to drift away." She paused, then looked back up at me. "Don't let your friend drown. But maybe don't go to see her alone."

18

Back on the 42 bus, and it was getting late. Connecticut Avenue was a mob of tourists on foot and in their cars (the ones with out of town plates were generally lost), and the bus driver made her way gladiator style through the rush. I hopped off on 14th and walked the few blocks up to my apartment. I was hoping for another evening of traveling to new places—that's what you're supposed to do with your significant other, isn't it? Travel? I thought about what Dr. Bel told me, and wondered who she was dating. Who goes out with a demi-goddess? Is there protocol? It just seemed stressful, is all. Before we went our separate ways, I told her to bring her beau to the bar, and she said she would do that, saying her partner was 'a bit younger than I am, we'd love to see where you work.' Since she's semi-immortal, that could be most of us. How old was she, anyway? That line of thought led me back to March. It occurred to me that instead of avoiding his time problem, maybe he ought to embrace it, like with allergy shots.

I came around the corner of my house and heard voices.

"...so you just sit there all day?" March asked.

"All damned day, man." A male voice. A young male voice.

Instead of being inside and asleep—or at least waiting for me alone, March was sitting on the back steps. Ray was a step below him, and Sheena was sitting with her legs crossed on the hood of my car. There were a couple of empty soda bottles, Sheena was working on a kombucha, and I spotted three beer cans lined up next to March, so they'd been chewing the fat for a while.

"Well, look who's at my house. Sitting on my car. Found out where I live, huh? What's up, guys?"

"They wanted beer, but I said no." March looked quite proud of himself.

"Good. That's really...what are you two doing here? Do your parents know where you are?"

Sheena rolled her eyes so hard she got a look at her own brain. "Dad's at work, and Ray's mom is at work too. They know we go out."

"I'll bet," I said. "So, what are we talking about?" I gave March a wide-eyed look of warning that I'm certain he missed. "Totally normal things, right?"

"Did you know they make these children sit inside? This school thing, you really need to ask what's happening there. It sounds awful." Ray nodded, and Sheena was gazing at March with a look I fully recognized.

"They have to go to school," I said, suddenly the voice of reason. "Or they—and their parents—will get in trouble." I had a vivid memory of 10th grade stoner Ruby coming home in the back seat of a Broward County Sheriff's Office car one hot afternoon. That ended my school-skipping career. "And it's getting late, so..."

"You didn't Brilo me," Ray said. "So we thought we'd come over and see what you found out."

"About Ms. Gonzales," added Sheena. "Also, how cool is it that your boyfriend is a unicorn?"

"Oh my God, March." Well, my dream of protecting them from xenos went south fast.

"She asked me," he said, like that solved everything.

I gave Sheena a hard, adult stare. "You asked him specifically. You said, 'Are you a unicorn'?"

"Well, sort of." She glanced at him. She didn't want to get him in trouble. "I asked him how you guys met."

"And I told them how you fended off three—no, four attackers and saved me, not half a mile from here." He caught my look of horror. "I told them the short version."

"It was so romantic," sighed Sheena.

"I guess it was cool," Ray admitted.

"He wouldn't show us, though. His unicorn self, I mean." She blushed.

I dropped my head in my hands. Then I looked back up. Time to get this train back on its wheels. Tracks. Whatever. "Okay. March, here, is a writer and definitely not a unicorn or any other mythical creature. It's his job to come up with crazy shi—stuff like this. He's got a short story in *The Atlantic*, maybe you—"

"You don't have to be like that," Ray informed me. "We know all about the xenos."

"My mom is obsessed with werefolk," said Sheena. "Her favorite show was *Real Housewolves* 'til it got cancelled." If I remembered correctly, one of the ladies ate her pool boy, and not in a good way. "So you don't have to be weird about March." She gave him that look again. "We understand."

"And he can help us find out about Ms. Gonzales. You got, like, powers, right?" Ray asked.

"Um," said March.

"We actually went to see her," I added quickly. "And she said she was fine and she wants to be left alone. She...you have to understand, she went through a really difficult...thing. She would super not be happy about me telling you what happened, and she needs time and some privacy. But she's fine."

"This look fine to you?" Ray passed me his phone. He'd shot the video from across the street and it was a little grainy, but it was plainly Marly—wearing her sunglasses—standing in the window, staring out. The timestamp read 10:43 PM. Two or three times, a light flashed in the room behind her. Was there someone else there? It might have been the reflection of a passing car. The video was over five minutes long and she never moved.

"Was this tonight? Before you came over?" He nodded. "Ray, man, you can't spy on people." I handed him back the phone and sighed. "Okay. She's in a pretty bad place. But I promise you guys I'm going to help her. She's my friend, and I won't let anyone—or anything—hurt her. And I know it'll work out, because after all, we have a unicorn on our side." Well, damn. That sounded pretty epic. "Now, March and I have some stuff to talk about. How are you two getting home?"

"Oh," said Sheena, "we can walk. It's not that far—"

"Nope," I said, and as I went to grab my keys my phone went off. It was a text from James. So this must all somehow be work related.

Out front. I'll see the children home.

"Your ride is here. Please promise me you won't spy on Marly any more, okay? We've got this." They reluctantly agreed

Sheena hoisted her backpack. "Promise me you'll be careful." That was definitely directed at March. I guess I was on my own. Then she looked my way. "Um, you didn't install Brilo, did you?" I admitted I was a little behind the curve. She laughed. "Ruby, just text him. Told ya, Ray. She's old."

Yep, absolutely epic.

Once the kids were safely in the back of the Rav 4, March and I spent a little while picking up the empties and straightening up. Funny how teenagers tornado through your place even when they only go inside to use the bathroom.

Later, we climbed into bed, and I told him about my conversation with Dr. Bel. "Can you tell me what you think is going to happen to me?"

I could see the frustration in his eyes. "I keep trying. I see blades. At least, I think that's what they are. Flashing silver. Or sometimes black. And I hear you crying out to me. But that's all." He rubbed his face. "I don't even know when, or if, you're really in danger at all. I'm sorry."

"Don't be. You didn't have to come back here. And if I really was in trouble, you're the one I'd call." I was starting to think it really had happened already. The hacksaw, that had flashed in the streetlight, and it had a black handle. That was burned into my memory, like every other part of the night we met. And I sure as shit cried out—I screamed my brains out, and so had Margaret. I put my head on his shoulder and he pulled me close. "Did you know you make magic happen around me?"

He looked over at me curiously. "Are you talking about the sex part?"

I laughed. "That's pretty magical, but no. Over the last few weeks, things have been moving around. My coffee cup. Books. They start floating around. I think it's because you're thinking about me." I felt like maybe leaving Sasha out of the conversation was the way to go. I was expecting him to either deny it or not understand me, but he nodded.

"I was. I wanted to let you know I was still there. I have to stop, of course. I'm sorry if it worried you."

He ought to think about signing his work. "I actually kind of liked it. But yeah, you'd better stop. Doctor Bel said doing anything magical could make you worse."

"This means we can't travel to the Elation Station anymore. I'm sorry."

Damn it! "Oh, honey, that's totally fine. There are lots of other things we can do together." I paused. "Are you okay with the fact that Doctor Bel and I talked about you?" I asked.

He smiled but didn't meet my eye. "Can I tell you something?" I nodded, bracing myself. "I kind of always assume everyone is talking about me."

I had to agree that made sense. "Hey I got you a present." I handed him a box wrapped in a plastic bag I'd stowed under the nightstand, and watched as he opened it.

"You got me a phone," he said. He didn't look as excited as I was expecting, or at all.

"Yeah, I mean, it's not as fancy as mine, but you can call and text on it. Look, I already put my number in there for you." He stared at it, rubbing his thumb across the smooth little glass window. "Is something wrong?"

He looked up at me. "I don't have any pockets," he said. "I mean, I won't. When I am myself again."

"Oh. Oh, I see. Um, well, you can leave it here, when you go back home. And I'll make sure it stays charged. In case you want to come back." I hadn't thought of that, the most obvious thing in the world. But my solution seemed to satisfy him.

"That's a good idea," he said. "I never had a phone before. Or a place to keep it. Thank you for both things."

That warmed my heart. It also warmed the rest of me, and I took the phone out of his hand before climbing on top of him and leaning in to kiss him. A phone, a bed, young people to care for, and me. It wasn't tricking him into wanting to stay if he wanted it, too.

Afterwards, we settled into sleep. Tucking myself against the curve of his shoulder felt like home, so comforting it took me by surprise. I obviously wasn't used to sleeping with people, but I found myself drifting off.

"I thought he looked familiar."

I sat up, completely awake. "What? Who?"

"Who what?" March blinked sleepily, I could see

faint light reflected in his eyes. "What's wrong?"

"You just said, 'I thought he looked familiar.'"

"No I didn't."

"You just did. Were you slipping?" I turned the light on. He held up his hand to shield his eyes.

"I was sleeping, I didn't say anything. I would remember if I did. You were dreaming. Come back here." He pulled me back into his arms. I reached over my head and turned out the light again. Who looked familiar? It could be anyone, or no one at all. Maybe I was dreaming. Eventually, I closed my eyes and this time nothing woke me up.

19

"Aello," said Shanti. She sipped her latte and nodded. "That's what you want to call a cautionary tale."

I pushed my eggs around the plate and flagged the waitress for more coffee. "Then you know who she is?"

"Sure," she replied. "And I'll tell you the story, but first—why? I mean, all of us—we harpies—we know the story, but other than that it's kind of obscure."

I'd been in such a hurry to find out who Aello was that I'd done a crap job of catching Shanti up. "It has to do with March. Lauren—in her notes—she mentioned Aello and made it sound like March was heading in the same direction." From the look on Shanti's face, I could see what that might mean.

"Oh. Oh shit, really?" She swung her braid back and fiddled with the elastic at the end, something she liked to do when she wasn't ready to get to the point.

"Well, Lauren was a smart girl, but she might have been wrong. I mean, she didn't say 'this is for sure going to happen to— "

I pulled out my phone and let her read the passage. She blanched.

"Is it that bad?"

More braid fussing. "It's...yeah, it's pretty bad." She took a breath. "Okay. This was when my folk were new. There weren't many of them, and they kept to themselves. I know, the Argonauts and all that—bad press. Anyway, the way I heard the story was, Aello was a favored daughter. She was a solid ten. The shiniest feathers, the sharpest claws, this girl had it. And one day she spotted a guy—I don't know, fishing or something. That's what mortal dudes did back then, right? So he was super cute. She was smitten. And I guess he must have given her the Grade A 'D' because she fell in love. So did he, which was nice. But she's at least goddess adjacent. She'll live a thousand times a thousand years."

"Wow, how old are you?"

"Rude bitch. I'm twenty-nine. Can I finish?" I nodded. "Anyway, she can't stand the idea of living without him, and she can't do anything about his brief mortal span. So she went to her mother Elektra and somehow convinced her to remove her gifts; her magic, her shape shifting, and her super long life. She turned herself into a mortal." She shook her head. "Elektra was a pushover."

That explained why Lauren was reminded of Aello. But I knew that wasn't the whole story.

"The end?" I asked. "Happily ever after?"

"Yeah, at first. But Aello wasn't meant to be a mortal. It's like she was wearing shoes that didn't fit. She got...the story isn't clear, its been retold so many times, but she got sick, and I always got the impression it was a mental disorder."

"What happened to her?"

Shanti sighed. "She died, Ruby. After staring at the bedroom wall for a couple of years. She died. I'm sorry."

I nodded. "Okay. But March didn't choose this. It wasn't his idea."

"Maybe it won't be the same." Shanti sounded hopeful. "After all, as we say the plural of anecdote is not data." I nodded sagely, like that had ever occurred to me. She continued. "Also that story is like, eight million years old. Half those tales are metaphors about not banging gods, right? This one could be the same thing, but in the other direction."

"A warning, not a diagnosis." I pondered this. A scary story the xenos told their children about the dangers of loving a mortal. "I hope you're right."

"So, how is it? With him being back?"

I sipped my coffee. "Confusing. Half the time, I'm sure of how I feel, and the other half, I'm thinking he's making me feel that way."

She gave me a shrewd look. "So he's making you

love him by being too loveable?"

"Ugh, not what I meant. He has this...power. He makes people love him. Quit acting like I'm making this up."

"He should be more like Sasha? A snotty pain in the ass? If you could love that bitch, it must be real? Am I wrong?"

She was trolling me at this point. "You aren't wrong. But we have to get his timeline straight before anything else."

She rolled her eyes. "Take it from a xeno who will live a long, long time—don't wait. You might get hit by a bus on the way home. He might lose his next fight with your fae friend. Or we could all get hit by a giant flaming meteor. Tell him how you feel. Isn't love supposed to be magic?" Her eyes widened. "Maybe that's the cure."

I shifted in my seat. "He's not Sleeping Beauty. This isn't a fairy tale."

"If it was," she said with a smile, "would you know?" Then she glanced at her phone. "I gotta blast. The two of you need anything, you let me know, okay?" She put a couple of bills on the table. "And give Sasha my love!"

I drank the rest of my coffee and rolled it around in my head. I had a fairy godmother in Dr. Bel, March was the cursed prince, Shanti was the good warrior, which made Sasha the cruel warrior...and Marly. A possessed princess? And me—I'd tried True Love's Kiss, True Love's Blowjob, and True Love's Mindblowing Fuck.

The only thing I hadn't tried was telling March the truth.

20

Turns out coming to a great realization is easier than following through. I wanted to tell him, I even opened my mouth, but I couldn't get the words out. Imagine blurting out, 'I love you,' to a unicorn. I mean, everyone loves him, right? Instead, I spent the afternoon at home, worrying. March promised he'd be careful and not do anything magical, and said he had some important errands to run. I made him practice calling me on his new phone and sent him out into the world. After a couple of hours of nothing happening, it was time to head to The Hare. Claudio and I huddled for a quick catch up session. Actually it wasn't that quick—the day before had been action packed. "Oh, and Sasha actually ate the Mega Slice. You owe me a dollar."

Grumbling, he fished it out of my tip jar and handed

it over. I let it slide. "So did you see anything interesting in Lauren's notes?" he asked.

"Yeah, a lot. She was, like, a scholar or something. That girl ran deep, and we had no idea."

"I did," Claudio said. I looked at him, surprised. "We talked about my finishing school—she was in favor, by the way—well, once she understood what I meant by school. She had more of an independent study thing going on. Why do you think she was writing on her hand all the time?"

I hung my head. "I thought she was just writing down what we were saying, I didn't know she was analyzing everything. Anyway, there wasn't anything about anyone threatening her. But we didn't get all the way through it."

"Did you start at the end?"

I gave a short laugh. "I should have put you in charge. No, we didn't. Damn, it sounds so obvious when you say it."

"Yeah, I'm full of good ideas. Like, I could have told you March would make an excellent babysitter. So where is he now?"

"Who, Sasha or March?"

Claudio rolled his eyes. "I forgot, you have a reverse harem—full of magical men. March, I mean. Sasha said he couldn't come in tonight."

"You are friends! That's so nice. Uh, March said he wanted to walk around and look at things. I guess we'll see him later?" I wondered what sort of errands a unicorn—a creature with no possessions (other than his new phone), no home, and no ties might do. I mean, he wasn't buying postcards of the Tidal Basin for his cousins back home in the enchanted glade.

Claudio brought me back to earth. "Closing remarks on the Marly situation?"

I sighed. "Still preparing them. You should have seen the video, Clo. She was just standing there, like, forever. She looked so lost. And all that stuff she said..."

"She didn't mean it, you know that, right? She's just..." He paused trying to think of what she could possibly be. "She's not herself."

"But if she won't let me in..."

"You'll figure it out. You said it yourself, you've got a damn unicorn on your side." He looked past me, at the door. "Also a team of supernatural women, it looks like. Hi, Doctor Bel."

Dr. Bel pulled up a stool, looking if possible even younger. She'd traded her updo for a sort of beachy tousled look. "Hello, Claudio, nice to see you again." Claudio and Dr. Bel (and by extension his grandmother in Brooklyn) were now good friends since I sat them together at Solstice dinner last winter.

"You, too. Oh, Nonna says thank you. She didn't have a fingernail of any saint at all, much less a really good one."

"Catherine of Siena was A-List, and I just had it

lying around. I'm glad she liked it. Um, guys, this is my friend Dafne. Even though she's lived here forever, she's somehow never been to The Hare. I figured I'd better bring her to D.C.'s finest drinking establishment."

Claudio politely laughed at her lame joke, and said 'hi' like a normal person. I just stared. The girl was tiny, gorgeous, and had the most amazing yellow-green eyes. It looked like she'd brushed the twigs out of her hair for her date, though.

"This is her?" said Dafne, who was staring back at me. "No way."

"I think we've met," I said. "Not officially." Of course, the little beauty next to Dr. Bel was the nymph from the apartment hallway. "I'm Ruby. Nice to meet you for real." I put my hand out, and after only a second's hesitation, she tapped her fingertips against my palm.

"Right," she said, looking around at the dim lights, exposed wiring, worn and scuffed wooden floor. "Nice place you got here."

"So you grew up here, huh?" Bless Claudio for spackling over the rough edges.

"I did," she said. "I live down by the river, at the Arboretum. That's my forest."

"She's a wood nymph," said Dr. Bel. "Did I already say that?"

"A wood nymph, that's cool." Claudio said. "Good choice of forests. I love that place."

"That's where we met," said Dr. Bel "I was in the

Bonsai exhibit, and we just started talking. Remember, Daf? It was that little, teeny bougainvillea." She laughed—a weird, trilling laugh—and I realized she was nervous. Alcohol to the rescue!

"What can I get you guys?" Dr. Bel ordered a Fernet, an Italian cordial which tasted like a mixture of gasoline and mouthwash, but I am told is very classy. When Dafne ordered, I laughed.

"Seriously?" She nodded with a glare that even Sasha would have to respect. "I'll have to look it up. No one's ever ordered a Grasshopper in here before."

She looked down her dainty nose at me (again) and said, "I have a sweet tooth." Right, of course. Every xeno I ever met had a sweet tooth. Then she paused, a slight smile on her face. "You *can* make one?"

"Yes," I laughed. "I am capable." I made the girl her drink.

"...and then they cut down all my lilacs." Dafne was complaining about the park service. "But they left me some choice offerings, and I'm happy to say everything is growing back. No thanks to them!"

"Offerings, huh?" I thought of Lauren and her gifts, and Sasha and his debts. "What do they leave you?"

Dafne got up off her stool like that little five-foot-nothing wafer of a girl wanted to come over the bar. Dr. Bel took her by the arm before she got too far. "Ruby doesn't know it's impolite to ask about that," Dr. Bel said quickly. "Isn't that right?"

"I did not know that." I held up my hands in surrender. "Apologies. No offense, I hope."

Tinkerbitch showed her perfect little teeth and sat back down. "None taken. But," and she looked back at Dr. Bel, "if this place is marked 'safe' she oughta know, don't you think?"

"Safe?" I asked. "For who?"

"For us. Xenos. For the xeno community. Didn't you know that?" Dafne looked from me to Dr. Bel. "How does she not know that?"

I smiled. "I guess I'm not on the mailing list." I tried to blow it off, but I had to wonder who put us there, and how many of my regulars were irregular. I'd have to turn the lights up and take a closer look.

"I mean, there's just stuff you should know. Like," Dafne continued, "you wouldn't ask a dragon about their horde, and you wouldn't ask a unicorn what time it is."

"It's a quarter to ten," said March, who had just come up behind her. "Are we telling jokes?"

I am willing to embrace my pettiness and admit a little pleasure in seeing the look on Dafne's face. "Dafne, this is my friend March."

"Your friend?" she sputtered.

"Also my friend," murmured Dr. Bel.

"He gets around," said Claudio.

"Oh, she's pretty," March said to Dr. Bel, who looked like she wanted to dematerialize. "She's the one you told me about!" He seemed delighted. "You know what? I think I know your cousin, the one from the tidal marsh near the ocean."

"Um," said Dafne.

"I'm sure it was her. Ondine? Something like that?" he mused as Claudio passed him a bourbon.

Dr. Bel cleared her throat. "March has just recently started thinking about the past," she said. "This may be a cousin from a really long time ago."

They started comparing notes: what March could remember (with a little assist from Dr. Bel) and whom Dafne was related to down in the Tidewater of Virginia. I looked around the bar: unicorns, nymphs, a demigoddess, and I was pretty sure the big guy nursing a beer by the window grew fur at least once a month. It struck me. This really was a xeno safe place. Once I had March (and Sasha and Marly) sorted, I was going to make it my business to find out who made that decision.

"Still not letting any vampires in," I said under my breath. As I went to make another round of Grasshoppers (they turned out to be so delicious everyone wanted one) my phone went off. It was texts from Marly.

I need to see you

not my house

Someplace safe

The bar was safe, a safe place for xenos, but that wasn't what she meant. I could only think of one place that truly qualified. If you weren't safe with a dragon guarding you, nothing could save you. I tried to type in the address, but I'd forgotten that Lauren's apartment was charmed against putting it in writing. I cursed at my phone and texted the closest intersection. I know Dr. Bel said I should think twice about seeing Marly alone, but I got her into this, and if I could, I was for fucking sure going to get her out.

I wrote:

meet me tomorrow at noon

I waited for the return text. Nothing.

"Hey, did you run out of crème de menthe?" called Dafne. I hustled to finish the drinks.

Two hours later, Dr. Bel and Dafne made their goodnights and left March at the bar. He was deep into his bourbon, and we were getting a look at another exciting new emotion.

He finished what was left in his glass and pushed it towards Claudio, who gave me a not-quite concerned look. I shrugged and he got his refill.

"Thank you," March said. Even when drunk and unhappy he was at least polite. He drank half of it in a gulp, and set it down a little harder than he probably meant to. "So this is what we do? What I do from now on? Good. I like this. I like it here. I don't have to do anything. Not that I'm allowed to."

"This isn't forever, babe." I reached across the bar and put my hand on his shoulder. "We'll figure this out."

"Will we? How?" He glanced up at me, and I have to say I didn't care for the look in his eye. I drew my hand back. "This is like before, only worse. Last time I couldn't be my true self even if I wanted to." He picked up his glass again and stared at it. "Now, I can either be myself or drown in time. I can't heal a child. I found out where she lives, but so what? Couldn't do anything but stand on the corner. I can't keep you safe. I can't..."

"March—" I began to say something that I hoped would calm him down. It didn't.

"What?" he snapped, this time slamming his glass on the bar. Bourbon splashed both our hands. His anger evaporated and he looked at me in shock. "What?" he repeated, but this time I could barely hear him. "What is this?"

I mopped both of us up with a bar rag. "Okay. Time to go." I promised Claudio we'd be fine and told him he could keep the whole night's tip jar, and I hustled March into a cab (no James, we were off duty). He sat slumped against the back seat, wordless. When the cab pulled up to my place, he followed me inside and headed for the bedroom.

"My skin is too tight." He sprawled on the bed without even taking off his sneakers.

I sat next to him. "You know, you're allowed to be angry."

He looked away, embarrassed. "It felt like a drop of poison in my blood, but the poison had come from my own hand. I didn't like it."

"I know. But you don't have to be ashamed of feeling things. Even bad feelings, even anger. Just think of who you're angry at."

He sat up. "I shouted at you. At you! I've said I was sorry before, but this is the first time I've ever actually felt sorry." He put a tentative hand on my arm. "I won't do it again."

"I believe you." I reached down and unlaced his shoes and pulled them off. "Is this really the first time you've ever yelled at someone?"

"I don't remember. And," he added with some bitterness, "I'm not allowed to go back and look." He sighed. "How do you mortals handle all...this?" He waved his hand. "All these feelings. Without magic, how do you stand it?"

"Alcohol and yelling. Welcome to it."

"I'm going to try and do better," he told me. "Less alcohol and absolutely no more yelling."

I got him a glass of water and some aspirin. It wasn't much, but it was all the mortal magic I could offer.

21

The next morning, I woke up in March's arms. I've never done that before—opened my eyes with someone's arms around me. I mean, I'm a light sleeper to being with, and then there was the years-long sex drought, so this felt important. He was already awake, hangover free, playing with my hair and gently rubbing my back.

"I like it here," he said. "I'm thinking I might want to stay."

"In bed?" Of course he meant in bed. What else could he have meant? "Okay then, let's not get up." I turned so I could see him but not so much that he'd get blasted with morning breath. "But first I have to brush my teeth and use the bathroom." Once I got myself under control—and put on just a little lip-gloss and ran a comb through my hair—I got back in next to him.

When we kissed, I wasn't even surprised that brushing his teeth was one more thing he didn't need to worry about.

"This reminds me," he said, nuzzling my ear and kissing my neck but not finishing his sentence.

I laughed. "Gonna tell me?"

"Oh, right. This reminds me of the cabin. We had a lot of sex there. I like to think about it."

"Me too," I agreed. "I still feel bad about arguing." I didn't want to bring up Gaia but I also wanted to get it off my chest. "I should have tried harder to understand you."

"That wasn't a real fight," he said. "We were manipulated by the *kitsune*. It is his trade."

"Ugh, that guy. I wonder whatever happened to him."

"Nothing good, I hope. And if he crossed Baba Yaga by telling us her name—or close enough to guess her name—I am certain that's exactly what he got."

"He was also supposed to deliver you to her poachers, so he screwed up twice." Technically he'd gotten that part right, but the poachers got interrupted—by me. I felt like Baba Yaga would be happy to blame the fox for that, too. I got a mean little shiver of satisfaction out of the thought of the smelly, nasty fox man facing the old witch.

"She takes things, you know." He said it like it was common knowledge.

"Takes things? What kinds of things?"

"Parts." I shuddered. "Remember she was going to take my heart. She took something from him. Something he will keenly miss."

I thought about the things he knew, about what was slowly surfacing in his memory, about the people and xenos he'd met.

"Tell me a story," I said. "About your life."

"A story?" He sounded dubious.

"Yeah." I sat up. "You started to tell me the other day. Outside the clinic. You said you once got caught."

"Oh. You really want to hear about that?" I nodded, and he pulled me back down so my head was on his chest. "It was a long time ago, but let me see if I remember. It was when I was living in what is now call France, the northern part, near the sea. The woods were endless and I went many years without seeing any humans. It occurred to me one day that I'd like to see some again, maybe even walk as one of them. I'd done it in the past and always enjoyed it. The idea consumed me. You should understand it might have been a dozen or more years from the time I thought of this to the time I did something about it. At last I found a small village that suited my idea of how human life should look, and I watched it. And in the spring of the year, I followed a young man and woman down to the shore. I spent days—I think it was days—following them as she gathered the berries that grew near the water, and he fished. They'd work in the morning, and make love on the sunny grass in the afternoon. Finally I let them see me."

"Did you look like you do now?"

"I have always looked this way." I could guess where this was going. He was about to poach the girlfriend.

"They saw me first in my own body, and then I showed them this one. People then didn't need the xeno community to reveal itself. We were there for them all along. They weren't surprised, but they were happy, as just catching a glimpse of one of my race was still rare enough for it to be great good luck." He gave a short laugh. "It did turn out to be good luck, for them. But here I was, sitting down to eat their bread and drink their wine. The boy was tall, and I remember his eyes were the color of the water. And she had long hair. Dark, like yours. But I can't recall their faces. I could try..."

"Remember what Doctor Bel said about magic. Won't it make you slip?"

"It would, if I went back there. So let's agree they were a handsome couple. We spent the season enjoying each other, we three."

Okay, I did not expect that. "That's hot." He buried his face against the back of my neck, laughing.

"Yes, it certainly was. So we passed the summer at our pleasure. But when the cold wind began to blow across the water, they came to the shore less frequently.

And then a peddler came through their town. That's how it began."

"That sounds ominous. How what began?"

"The sickness. It wasn't the Black Death, it was just a little plague the man brought with him from the south, but it hit my village hard. The young woman came to the shore one day, looking for me. 'Are you well?' I asked her, although I could see she was not sick, only distraught. She kissed me and said, 'I know you can heal the sick. I know what your kind can do. He is sick, he will die. As you love him, you must save him.' I didn't tell her I didn't love him, for how could I love a mortal?"

Well, there it was. At least I knew. I was glad he couldn't see my face. He continued with his story.

"I didn't love him, but neither did I wish him dead. I knew it was dangerous for me to show myself to so many people, but I had the means to help him, and I agreed to go with her. And I followed her through the forest, up the path to the road leading to the village. Everyone who lived there came out to watch me pass. Even wearing the body of a man, they knew what I was. I imagine she told them she'd find help, and she did. I think it's possible she was proud of the fact that she alone was able to call one of my kind to her side. It's also possible I was also proud, that I alone could save him. She led me to the boy's bed, and in my sadness at seeing him weak and suffering I put aside my fear and let them all see my real form. You know I can't cure a malady when I'm like this. So I touched him, and I healed him. He sat up, and his blue eyes were bright. 'Thank you,' he said. 'Thank you,' she said. 'And I am sorry.' Standing next to her was a younger girl, maybe her sister. She held out her hand."

"They got a virgin."

"They did. There were more sick people, so many more, and they couldn't allow me to leave."

"But how did they get you to stay? That girl couldn't have kept her hand on your 24/7, like she was trying to win a car." He didn't know what that meant, of course, but let it pass without comment.

"They had planned for this. And so they cut off the virgin's hand and used it to hold shut the door."

"WHAT?" I sat up so fast I whacked him in the chin with the top of my head. "Is that true? Ugh, sorry." I rubbed my head, and he ran his finger along his jaw.

"Maybe they had a silver psalter in their church, blessed by the pope in Rome himself, and melted it down to forge a shackle."

"Which one is it?"

"It might have been the witch who lived by the shore, who spied on us and was jealous of our play. She cursed a bunch of wicker wythes, and so they built a cage."

"You don't remember." I leaned against him again.

"I think all of those things happened. Not all at

once. I don't know which one. Anyway, they held me there for...it was a long, dark season, and cold. The only window was set up near the roof. I could only see the moon as it passed. I had hay for a bed—I suppose that's what they thought I would choose to sleep on. And there was work for me every day. People brought their sick children, their brothers and mothers and lovers, and even if I wanted to, I couldn't refuse. And then one day when the vines began to send green shoots across the window ledge and into my cell, the young woman came to me and found me poorly. However they restrained me made me weak and tired, and seeing so many sick mortals made my heart ache for the freedom of the forest, and for solitude. 'People are on their way from the city to see you,' she said. 'A caravan of the infirm, I have heard. Many more than before.' I told her I wouldn't be of much help, that soon I'd be a white goat, or an unusually large and pale-hued carp. 'I don't know if you're lying,' she said, 'but I know I have mercy to repay in kind.' And she let me go. I left and didn't look back. I don't know what happened to her, or her village. It was a hundred years and more before I saw another human face."

"I'm glad she set you free," I said. I put my arms around him and made a promise to myself—that even though he could never love me it didn't mean I didn't love him. And I wouldn't be the one to lock him in another cage.

22

Finally, we did have to get up. It was almost time for my appointment with Marly. I had just enough time to run a few errands. The grocery store first. Coffee, half-and-half, a splurge on a bottle of wine that cost more than eleven dollars, black beans, pasta, a box of doughnuts. I dropped off my laundry and put the doughnuts next to March where he was planted in front of the TV.

"I'm going to try and talk to Marly," I told him.

He looked up. "Do you need me?"

"No, I think it's got to be just the two of us. I think she wants to explain why she's been acting...what's going on. But you have your phone, so I'll be in touch."

He motioned at the screen. "I think they're going to go for the third house. It's got closet space and a white kitchen." What was it with xenos and reality shows?

I bent over and kissed the top of his head. "Just keep your phone on."

After that I headed down to the corner off of Dupont Circle. I got there early—I got everywhere early, it's a sickness—and passed the time by pacing and assuming Marly wouldn't show up.

"Can we go inside?"

Marly had snuck up behind me, wearing the ever-present sunglasses, along with stained long-sleeved t-shirt and equally grubby sweatpants. She didn't smell like garbage—and she was standing in the sun under the open sky—but she didn't smell exactly daisy fresh, either. I got her down the alley, and she spent as much time looking over her shoulder as she did at the chain link fence and tagged old brick walls. Once I blew on the door and the real, cheery and inviting walkway and building appeared, I heard her say 'huh' to herself. The door troll greeted me with his usual terrifying snaggle-fanged grin and was about to say hello, but when he caught sight of Marly, his smile vanished, and he took a step back.

What was she, that could make a troll back down?

I let her into Lauren's apartment—I'd texted Sasha and he informed me he was 'out' and 'don't touch my things' which for him seemed like a love note and a dozen roses—and turned on the lights. She headed straight for the fridge and pulled out a box of half eaten chocolate cake. I watched as she rummaged through the drawers, found a spoon, and began to eat right out of the carton. I couldn't tell for sure, but her teeth looked like regulation teeth. As she ate, she went to the window and pulled the blinds, and then made sure no one was in the bedroom.

"Are you going to take those glasses off?" I asked. She shook her head. "Are we going to act like you never said all that shit to me?" She shook her head and kept eating

Finally, I'd had it. "Mar, if you're not going to talk to me, why did you text me? What's going on with you? You look like boiled ass!"

Finally finished, she put the empty carton on the counter and spoon in the sink. "I had to make sure he wasn't following me. He can get in anywhere. He doesn't believe in doors."

"He who? Sasha?" I cocked my head at her. "When did you even meet him?" She shook her head 'no' and I noticed she was kneading her hands together. They looked busted. "What the hell happened to your hands?"

She snatched them behind her back. "Not Sasha. He's the fae, right?" I nodded. "Yeah, I've heard of him. No. Someone else. He...won't go away. He won't leave me alone. Is he from you? Or the fae? Make him leave me alone, please."

"Mar, I don't know who you're talking about. Who is 'he'?"

"He found out I'm...wrong. I lock my door and he comes in. I hide, and he finds me. I can't...he won't leave me alone. He was gone this morning, and that's how I got out." She rubbed her hair back out of her face and I got a better look.

"Honey, let me see your hand." I reached for her, but she yelped like I smacked her and pulled away. "What's wrong with you?"

"I don't know," she whispered. "It's in my blood. An anomaly. I don't know what's happening to me. My hands..." she held them up. They looked burned. Not like sunburned, like picked up a hot frying pan burned. "They hurt. My throat hurts. My eyes..."

"I'm calling Doctor Bel." To my relief, she nodded shakily, and I whipped out my phone. "Can you sit down? No one is getting in here. Whoever this dickbag is, we'll find him and make him stop, okay?" I sent out a group text asking everyone to come over, figuring we'd better take advantage of her being willing to talk. And maybe one of my xenos would know who or what was doing this to her. "Okay, she'll be here in a couple of minutes. So just try and relax." She rested her forehead against her hands, and whispered something. "I didn't get that," I said.

"I'm sorry." Her voice was thick and gluey. "About what I said. He made me say it. I know the vamp thing wasn't your fault. I was just so pissed at you." A tear rolled out from under the oversized glasses and dripped off her chin. "And then I wanted to call you, but he kept hiding my phone and telling me I was right to be mad, it should have been you, all this bullshit. He hates you, and he wanted to make sure I hated you, too." She sniffled. "For a little while, it worked." She lifted her glasses just enough to wipe her eyes. "But last night I managed to sneak my phone into the bathroom, and that's when I texted you. He took away the door right after. Then today, I don't know where he was. I got out. I don't know if he followed me. I'm so tired..."

I put my hand over hers, careful of her scorched fingers, and gently squeezed. She didn't flinch away so I left it there.

"Who is this guy? Does he have a name?"

She shook her head. "If he told me, I don't remember. I can't...I can't remember what I'm doing half the time. And," she barked a laugh, "I keep smelling this gross, cat-piss smell. Now I know how you must have felt, right?" I flinched. If she started on me again, I didn't know how I'd react. But I let her continue. "I don't know if he smells, or if there's no him at all and I'm imagining it. He keeps telling me I've done bad things. Bad things, really bad. But is he in my head? I don't know." My own, human blood turned cold. I forced myself to look at the blackened, crisped burns on her hands, her stained shirt, the sunglasses. It killed me to consider it, but maybe she wasn't hallucinating, and maybe March didn't bring her back all the way. "Maybe

I am bad. Maybe I never really *wasn't* a vampire. March shouldn't have bothered with me."

Her voice cracked. She was crying. Vampire, killer, lunatic or victim, this was still my friend, and I wouldn't let her drown.

"Marly, oh my God, no. He brought you back because it was the right thing to do, and we will figure this out. "I wanted to throw my arms around her but I didn't want to hurt her. "I've missed you so much," I said. "I love you. I'm going to fix this."

"I love you too," she whispered. "But maybe you should stay away from me."

No. She wouldn't hurt me. Would she?

Then she looked at me, or she looked in my direction. "Um, would you see if there's more cake or cookies or something in the fridge?"

"You could eat?"

I got a hint of a ghost of a smile from her. "Yeah, I could eat."

I squatted down in front of the fridge and found a tube of chocolate chip cookie dough. "This is gross but we can share it—" I straightened up and looked over the kitchen island.

The door stood open. Marly was gone.

"Shit, goddammit, Mar!" I chucked the plastic tube back in the fridge harder than I meant to, and an avalanche of leftovers fell out; pizza, cheese, tubs full of whatever Lauren would never get to finish. Along with the remains of our pizza, the magical paper evidence bags came tumbling out, and I tried to catch them on their way down. Sasha would be pissed if they got ruined. Too late—I grabbed one too hard and it split open, dumping its contents among all the other crap on the kitchen floor. It was full of orangey-red hair. No. Fur. Stinky red fur. Fox fur.

A persuasive, nasty man who smells like cat piss and sometimes has long, red fox fur.

I lock my doors and he comes in. He won't leave my house. He can get in anywhere...

I punched a number into my phone.

"Ruby? Is something wrong with Ms.—"

"Ray, can you do me a favor? Can you send me the video of Marly?"

"But you said..."

"I know what I said but I need it. It could be really important. Please, can you send it right now?"

He said he would, and we clicked off. Thank God we both had good service, because it only took a couple of minutes to download. I watched it again, and when the light I'd noticed flashed onto the screen, I paused it and expanded it. It was no passing car.

"Shiiiit." It was just an outline, a shadow against the drapes, but now that I bothered to really look I could see it was the outline of a tall, skinny man, holding a glowing, lighted ball up to his face. You could even almost make out his red hair. It was the *kitsune*. And

Marly was headed right back to him. I thought about waiting for Dr. Bel to arrive, or Sasha, or March, but I didn't. I couldn't. I let her go, and now I had to go get her back. I hit the street, bounced into the car, and asked James how fast he could get to Columbia Heights.

It turned out to be pretty fast.

23

"This is stupid, this is so dumb," I kept repeating it like a new, less-affirming mantra. Surprisingly, the front door to Marly's building was unlocked, and that has literally never happened before. She must have been in such a hurry to get home that she didn't make sure it latched behind her. I'd been psyching myself up to kicking it in, or breaking the glass with a rock or something. I didn't know whether the door being unlocked was good or bad.

Only one way to find out.

I figured the *kitsune* had been asleep—I saw him sleeping once, so I know he sleeps—and that's how Marly escaped. Then, when he discovered she was gone, he went hunting and found her with me. She must have sensed he was near, why else would she have bolted like that? The only other reason was that she was afraid she was going to hurt me. But even if she ran because she was afraid of what she might do, she didn't actually do it. She came to me for help. Now it was on me to find her. She was so lost and hurt, where else would she go but back home?

"Really, really dumb, Rubes," I reminded myself as I climbed the three flights to her floor. The only weapon I had was my garlic spray, so I may have been dumb, but at least I wasn't unarmed. That shit was strong. It didn't have an effect on Sasha, but the *kitsune* was no fae warrior. I felt like if I got the drop on him, I might be able to pull this off. I started planning. I would get Marly hidden in the bathroom or behind the couch, and I would get him while he was coming through the door—I could put him on the ground. Then all I had to do was grab his lighted ball, the thing that stored his soul, or mojo, or whatever. I'd done it once before, with March, who distracted him while I snatched it up. Then I could worry about getting Marly some help. I gripped my spray in one hand and my phone in the other.

Her door was open, and the lights were out. I thought about what I found at Lauren's unlocked, darkened apartment. "Really stupid," I muttered, and pushed the door fully open. A couple of things happened.

From behind the door, a shape—a tall, cat-piss smelling shape—leapt out, knocking the spray out of my hand. I dove over the couch and headed for the kitchen, thinking *knives, knives,* but the skanky fucker was too fast and cut me off. I saw the faint outline of the bathroom door, and threw myself onto the floor and slid inside. I got the door shut, but of course most old buildings in D.C. now don't have locks on the interior doors. I sat with my back against the frame and my feet braced against the tub. He hurled himself at the door, and it shook, but didn't blow open. He may have been tall, but he was stringy. He probably only had fifty pounds on me.

"Where's Marly, you little bitch?" I yelled. With or without her being in on it, he'd set a trap for me. Sometimes I really hated xenos.

He gave a snarly burst of laughter. "Oh, this must be the part where you follow her home to rescue her. Well, I'm afraid she isn't here. Poor crazy thing must have gotten lost. Well, I let her go, she'll come back. She has nowhere else to go, right? Me and Marly, we're practically roommates now, I guess you've heard. We share everything. Like how all her friends abandoned her. Like how she's a dirty, nasty, bad girl." He made normal comments sound gross, so this was obviously super disgusting.

"Are you still pissed that we stole your ball last year?"

"Oh, you know what? I'd almost forgotten about that." Yeah, he was still pissed.

"Did you kill those people?" I knew he killed Lauren—I saw the evidence all over the kitchen floor—but it would buy me some time, and I knew from experience how much he loved to talk. I wiggled around on my butt so I could fish my phone out of my back pocket...where it wasn't, because it fell out of my hand when I hit the floor. I figured it was under the stove by this point. *Really, really dumb.*

"Oh, you mean that fae chick? Maybe I did...or maybe it was my dear sister Marly. She'd do it, too. She's been doing lots of things, lately. Bad, bad Marly." He laughed, more softly this time, but at least he wasn't pounding on the door. "Oh, and by the way, I'm pretty sure Marly must have told you one very special thing about me."

"You stink?"

"Haha, charming. No. See, the thing about me is, I don't believe in doors."

And the door was gone. I was crouched right up against his legs. I looked up just in time to see him swinging the iron bar over his head, and again I dove out of the way. It missed cracking my skull, but connected with a loud 'thump' against the meat of my bicep. I howled like I was the wild animal in this scenario and scuttled behind Marly's lone armchair.

Catching my breath, I glanced around the corner. The bathroom door was back. But the front door—the only way out—was gone. There was just a blank wall.

Marly was right, there was no way to keep him out.

"I've been waiting for this for a long time. To give you what you deserve." He laughed, and it sounded like barking. "And we've got all day." He poked at me with the bar—I think it was a fireplace poker—but only halfheartedly. I realized he knew he could take his time. No one was coming, he wouldn't be interrupted. He wanted to play. "You ruin everything you touch."

"I'm not the one tormenting a sick girl, you disgusting freak." One day I'd learn to keep my mouth shut, but this was not that day.

He hissed with anger. "This is because of you. She did this because of you." He pushed back his shaggy red-orange hair, revealing a ragged mass of scar tissue running from behind his jaw up into his hair, and a knot of mottled red and white skin that used to be his ear. "She wanted to take my tongue but changed her mind. She said she might need it again."

March was right—she had taken something. I was too shocked by the sight of his destroyed ear to make a run for it, not that there was anywhere to go. "Ouch, nasty!" I said. "Cut yourself shaving?"

"Baba Yaga did this, you dumb bitch. I sold her out to you and your fucking horse. She wasn't amused."

"How is it my fault that your boss is a psycho? She hurt me, too, right?"

"Oh, boo fucking hoo, she hurt you. You look fine. Look at me!" I did. His face was distorted with rage, spittle flew as he spoke. "What's a fox with one ear? Useless. Nothing. This is on you. You stole my *ball*." He punctuated the last word with a vicious jab of the poker, and I rolled out from behind the chair and under the coffee table, but not before the sharp point caught and tore open the leg of my jeans. The low table wasn't wide enough to get all the way under it, so I had to crab crawl away from him.

"You know how hard it was to set this up?"

"What? Set what up?"

"Why do you think I spent all that time with your crazy friend? For kicks? Well, that's actually true. But hurting her was also hurting you, and hurting you was as good as sticking a knife in your horse." He strolled as he talked, jabbing the poker at my exposed legs. "You don't get to ruin me and then just fucking walk away!" The bar slammed into my knee and skidded down my leg, tearing off a strip of skin the entire length of my shinbone. The room went black with spinning silver stars, and I screamed. He took advantage and pounced, grabbed my bleeding leg and hauled me out from under the table. I tried to twist away, my leg was slippery with blood, but he already had one hand over my mouth, and the bar was jammed across my throat. The dirty taste and smell of his hand filled my sinuses and I couldn't take a breath. He may have been skinny, but he was strong. I scrabbled at the poker, but my hands were getting numb. I couldn't move. In a couple of seconds, it would be over. I could see the window, I could see the lights going out.

I'm going to die, I thought, *just like Lauren. Just like Dr. Mike. I'm sorry, Marly...I'm sorry, March...March... help me...*

The light came back. The pressure vanished. I took a huge gulping breath and tried to spit the taste away. The *kitsune* wasn't behind me anymore. I didn't know where he was, and I didn't want to wait and see if this was another game. My leg was on fire, my neck throbbed, my arm was numb, and I had just about got my feet under me when I heard his growling, rasping yelp. He was back where he'd started, next to the reappeared front door. The bar was pressed against his throat, pinning him in place with invisible hands a foot below the ceiling. I could see threads of steam rising from the flesh where the iron bit into it.

"Get it off me," he whined.

"Bullshit I will," I croaked.

He managed to get his fingers under it, and it slowly tore away from his neck, bringing with it strings of partially cooked flesh. Then he looked up at me and screamed.

"What the fuck?" I turned to see what was behind me. He wasn't looking at me, he was looking past me, at the kitchen. At the knives. All the knives: cleavers and carvers, poultry shears and tomato slicers, a complete set of horn-handled steak knives I got Marly as a housewarming present. All the blades. Dead black and bright, winking silver, hovering in mid-air. All pointing at him. When they started to move, I hit the floor and they hissed as they shot over my head.

When it was over, he was pinned like a butterfly to the wall. Most of the blades missed his skin. He was swearing in a language I definitely did not know, and his hands were halfway back to being fox paws. I wondered if he managed to change completely, if that would set him free.

I climbed up the side of the couch and dragged my bleeding leg behind me to the kitchen. "Gotta make a call," I said, blinking hard against the black and white shimmers that threatened to block out the light. "Gotta sit down, but making a call first."

"Who the fuck are you talking to? Who are you calling?" The *kitsune* writhed in his knife prison, but couldn't transform or escape. It looked like I was safe for a minute.

"Nunya," I said. He cocked his head at me. "Nunya business!" It was Claudio's nonna's favorite joke, and I laughed at myself so hard I finally did sit down—actually kind of slowly collapse—wheezing, onto the kitchen floor. I took a deep breath and willed my head to stop spinning. Then I called the number.

"Hi, it's Ruby, I'm the one who—oh, you knew that. Okay. I have something for you. Come get it, like, right now please." I texted the address and settled down to wait, holding a dishtowel to my leg and struggling to sit upright.

"How did you do that trick? With the knives?" The *kitsune* had calmed down some and sounded genuinely curious.

"I didn't do it. I'm a regular mortal, remember?"

He narrowed his yellow eyes. "Someone did. Someone protects you." He paused, "He's still powerful, even if he is dying." He snickered. "Lauren's notes were so enlightening."

"He won't die. I won't let him." Why was I arguing with him? *Magic, March did magic*. It seemed important, but I couldn't remember why.

"Well, he won't have another chance. He should have killed me just now, while he still had his wits about him. He cares whether you live or die, and when I get free, I'll make sure he lives long enough to see me slit your throat."

"He won't get that chance. Will you, fox?" Standing in the doorway was the dragon.

"Tha." I slowly got to my feet. "We got him." Then it got dark again. That's what happens when you pass out.

24

I opened my eyes and found myself on Marly's couch with my leg up on the coffee table. I gathered that while I was away, Tha moved me here and wrapped my leg in a towel, which was spotted with blood.

"You're back. Good. I have work for you." Tha set aside the knitting she'd been working on, and leaned forward.

"I think I need to go to the emergency room," I said.

"It's not as bad as it looks," she said, not helpfully. "Can you stand?"

Slowly, trying to surf the waves of nausea and lightheadedness, I stood up. My leg throbbed. I didn't think my arm was broken, but I could barely lift my hand. My neck ached. I was just getting used to not having anything weird going with my throat, too. Oh well. "What do I have to do?" I asked.

"Die screaming, you miserable cow. Bleed out on the fucking floor." The *kitsune* chimed in from the wall where he still hung, dripping his own blood onto Marly's hardwood.

Tha smiled thinly. "I'm pleased you woke up. He," she jerked her head back, "likes to run his mouth. You and I, we'll take care of that." She told me what she wanted me to do, and it sounded simple at first. All I had to do was take away his ball. Again.

"And when you've gotten the soul ball away from him, I'll take it off your hands. He'll be my responsibility." She glanced in hi direction. "He was a terrible tenant. Let's see how he works out as a pet."

The *kitsune* was sounding a little frantic, "They're using you, Ruby. Why are you trusting any of them?" He made a sharp, barking sound. "Oh! Your bar—the safe space. Who made it so? And why?"

"Because shut up," I said, even though I was wondering that same thing myself. To Tha I said, "Well, okay. How do I find out where he's keeping it?"

He laughed. "You'll see. You'll wish I was there to help you. You'll end up alone, none of them care about you. You're just a mortal—"

"Tha, where's the damned ball?"

She smiled again. "He keeps it tucked behind his most valued possession."

Why was I trusting her? "If it's his balls I'm out."

She made a *psssht* noise. “His tongue, girl. It’s down his throat.”

Now he leered at me. “Come to me, Ruby. Put your fingers in my mouth. I want you to.”

I glanced nervously at him as he waggled his tongue at me. Gross. “Um, I don’t guess you can do it?”

She shrugged. “I could only reach up that high if I brought out the dragon, and I can’t promise he’d survive that meeting. You must take the ball, and then I will take the captive.”

“But the king said—”

“Take your time, ladies,” the *kitsune* said from his spot near the ceiling. “Ruby, that leg looks pretty bad. I bet you’re dying!”

She glanced at him. “We do this now, together.” She stood. “I will help you.” She dragged the kitchen chair she’d been sitting on to where he hung, suspended. I guess I was supposed to stand on it and not fall off and break my other leg.

“Thanks.” I half-hopped, half-dragged myself over to the kitchen and rummaged through Marly’s utensils—the ones that weren’t stuck into the *kitsune*, that is—and found the one I was looking for. I climbed awkwardly up on the chair, balancing on my good leg. “Open wide, champ.” I raised the barbeque tongs, long as my arm, and held the nice, sharp, serrated edge up to his face. “I suggest you don’t move around too much. Wouldn’t want to cut your tongue out. Like Baba Yaga said, you might need it one day."

He bared his teeth, and then sneered, "You will regret this. I'll remind you of this moment. This will not go unanswered."

"Whatever." I thought about Marly, about how he'd hung around her like a bad smell, how he'd tried to make her believe she'd done terrible things. How he blamed me. How he'd murdered Lauren and that poor doctor. Then I paused. "You killed Lauren because she knew something you didn't want me to find out. What was it?"

"If I tell you, will you let me go?"

"No," I said. "Even if I wanted to, Tha has already claimed you. You won't leave this room. So you might as well tell me."

Then he smiled, his eyes glittered. "Ask the king, when you see him." Then he opened his mouth. It looked like he swallowed a flashlight. I tossed the barbeque tool aside and went and got some rubber coated tongs and went after his soul. He didn't budge. I wiped the slime off the thing—now a glowing ball the size of a walnut—and handed it to Tha. She put the ball into a Ziploc and put it in her knitting bag, and then pulled a leather collar and leash out of her coat pocket. The *kitsune* began to whine like a scared dog, which I guess he sort of was, and I admit I felt a little sorry for him. Tha didn't strike me as an indulgent pet owner. She held the leash up with one hand and snapped her fingers with the other. Now that she had his ball, she controlled his powers, but he got one last shot in. He looked at me and said, "The king knows. You ask the king who put Lauren in my path," and then he melted away, out of his clothes and back into a fox—maybe slightly larger than normal, but nowhere near as big as the last time I'd seen him. A big fox with one missing ear. He held himself stiffly as she slipped the collar over his head.

She gave the leash a shake. "Come along." He lowered his head and followed her meekly to the door. "Thank you, Ruby," she said to me. "This was mercifully done. One of my kind would not have hesitated to incinerate this creature. I hope you don't regret your kindness."

It wasn't my kindness, though. If it had been up to me one of those knives would have been buried in his neck.

After she'd gone, I sat on Marly's couch, which was already so bloodstained I figured a little more wouldn't add that much to the dry-cleaning bill. I had a hundred and forty-seven messages, but they'd have to wait. First, there was someone I had to talk to.

"Marly?"

"Y...yes...are you okay?" Her voice was a raspy whisper.

"I'm okay. I need to tell you something."

"I'm sorry I left like that, but I was afraid I'd do

something..."

"I got him." There was a long pause. I could hear conversations in the background, and chiming bells.

"What?"

"I got him. He was real. You never hurt anyone. I got him, and I took away his soul. He's gone." I could hear her sniffle, she started to cry. "Where are you?"

"I'm on the Metro. I've just been riding around."

"Can you get to Lauren's apartment? I need to see you. March will be there." I was crying too. "There are so many people who love you who want to see you. It's gonna be fine."

I took a minute to get my head clear, leaning forward with my elbows on her coffee table. The blood on my hand dripped onto the scattered papers, and I pushed them away. Or I started to. I sat up slowly.

Blood work results requested by Dr. Michael Kennedy for patient Marly Gonzalez.

I didn't know what the rows and lines of numbers meant, or why so much of it was in red, but there was one word I did recognize, and it was repeated over and over. *Anomaly.* I folded the sheet and shoved it in my pocket.

I looked around Marly's trashed apartment, at the blood—two different people's worth—all over the floor and the couch, the knives still forming the outline of a body, clothes hanging limply on the wall. *Ask the king, when you see him.* It may be fine, but it wasn't yet. I shut the door and limped slowly toward the stairs.

25

"I'm really sorry," I said to James. "I'm getting blood all over your back seat."

"Don't worry about that." He looked away from the rear-view mirror as he turned onto 14th Street. "I feel like I would be remiss if I didn't strongly recommend medical care."

"Doctor Bel's a doctor," I said, "So that counts." I watched the king's silver medal slowly spin on its silk cord. Tree/cloud/dragon/cloud/tree/dragon/cloud.

"Ruby? Are you with us?" He was watching me in the rear view again and looked pretty worried.

"Huh? Oh. Yeah. I'm fine." I must have fallen asleep. It was hard to keep my eyes open, hard to try and sit up, so I didn't try.

"We are here. I'm going to help you inside, all right?"

I nodded. My tongue felt thick. He half supported, half carried me up the pathway, past the wide-eyed troll, and into the elevator. When we got to Lauren's door, he said "I think its best I leave you here. They're inside and they will take care of you."

I hugged his neck and watched him go. The door was open, I guess I opened it. I stood in the doorway. March was there. He jumped up, he was reaching for me. That was nice of him.

I opened my eyes. I was stretched out on the couch, this time it was Lauren's couch. Not her couch anymore, though. Sasha and March were looking down at me. "Hi guys."

"Hi." March knelt next to me and said, "Would you give us a minute?" Once Sasha was gone he unpinned the towel. "You won't like this." Some of my blood had dried, and the fabric was stuck to me. As he gently worked it free, he said, " Doctor Bel will be up in a minute. Where is Marly? I thought she was with you."

I shook my head and gritted my teeth, the pain helped me focus. "She'll be here—ow! No, keep going."

He set the towel aside. My knee looked like a purple and green softball and the poker had peeled off an inch-wide strip of skin all the way down my shin. I got queasy and looked away. "I can help you here, I think."

"You're going to speed it up."

"You remembered."

"March, you can't. It's magic. You aren't supposed to— "

"Are you ready?"

Before I could say no, he put his hands on my knee and a jolt of white agony shot down my leg. I didn't even have time to scream before the pain was gone. So was most of the swelling. It was still colorful, but it was definitely better. And not only had the bleeding stopped, but the gash on my shin was scabbed and shiny with new pink skin. It's hard to describe, but my leg felt warm and happy. Yeah, my leg felt high. Does that make sense? He repeated the action—warm, gentle touch, eye-watering pain, then peace and quiet—to my bruised shoulder.

"You fixed me," I said. I might have been a little punchy. "Now do my neck."

"Can't," he said. "Everybody only gets two." At the look on my face, he smiled. "That was a joke."

"Oh, ha." Everybody's a comedian.

"You don't know me, do you? I'll find a way to make this right. I'll never forget you." His eyes were unfocused. He was slipping. He'd only *just* done magic—the knives, and then my leg, and it already started. I took a second to wonder who he was talking to, and then gently shook him.

"Honey, come back. March, come on. Come back to me."

He blinked twice. "Sorry, I was trying to make you laugh. It was dumb. Come here. Let me see." Wherever he went, he came back just as quickly. He sat next to me and pulled me into his lap. "I won't have my best work ruined." He pushed my hair back and examined my neck.

"How does it look?"

"Like a bruise." He paused, his brows drawn together. "Like it hurts. All of this, every bad thing. Pain. Because of me. I've dragged you into such dark places." He shook his head and took a breath. "Let me at least fix this."

"I'll try and not get my neck torn up again. Promise. Ow!" Like before, a sharp blast of pain, and then warmth and peace. I leaned against him. "I insist you keep dragging me around by the way. I'll let you know when something's your fault." I laughed. "Drag me, baby." Definitely punchy.

"I just don't understand why you're happy to see me."

I touched his cheek. "You left your home—left your body—because you thought I might be in trouble. And you were right. It was you, at Marly's house. Wasn't it?"

He nodded. "I heard you call me, you called my name and you needed my help. It happened as I saw, except all along I thought the blades would be pointed at you." He shook his head. "You were foolish to go there alone. If you expect me to drag you into danger, don't you think you ought to do the same for me?"

"Sounds almost like you're sticking around." Warning lights were flashing in my brain, but my mouth apparently didn't care. "You want to be human with me for a while?" *He did magic, he's going to slip away from you...*

"I have to make sure you don't get into trouble." He smiled, he was so beautiful. "Who else is going to take care of your neck?"

"I love you." It just came out. Swear to God I wasn't planning it. He looked at me with wide, wondering eyes. "Oh my God. I'm sorry. Jeez, um. Blood loss, right?"

"Is that what this is? I didn't know it had a name. It feels better than alcohol and yelling. Love. I like it." When he kissed me, I almost fainted again, but in the best possible way.

26

We **had a good few** minutes, after that. Nothing hurt too much, no one slipped through time or got knives flung at them. No one died, or cried (I might have cried a little), and it was just us, just me wrapped in March's arms. We kissed for a while.

"It's been a long time since I said that to anyone," I told him. "I was afraid you'd be...I don't know. Put off."

He pondered that. "Since I met you, I've had a lot of new things to think about. Phones. Cars. Last week. Last year. Love is probably the nicest. But I don't know how 'put off' feels."

I decided not to borrow trouble by explaining that if you said 'I love you' to someone—if you did it too soon—it made them leave. "Then it doesn't matter. But we still have to fix your time problem. Maybe Doctor

Bel—" The door opened, and there she was, like I'd summoned her. She had her hand firmly under Marly's elbow as she led her into the room, and Shanti came right behind them. I quickly put my feet on the floor, and we straightened our clothes. Well, I did. March hadn't learned to be self-conscious, and if it was up to me he never would.

"And I thought she looked bad," Shanti looked from Marly to me. "Girl, you look like hammered shit." Shanti put her hands on her hips. "When this is over, I'm taking you both to the spa—the nice one with the hot rock rooms."

When I got up to hug her, my knee gave a twinge, but that was it.

I turned to Marly. "How are you feeling?" I asked her.

"I didn't kill anyone, and he's gone. So still shitty, but better?"

"You ever gonna take those glasses off?"

She jerked her head to one side. "Nuh...not yet. No." I nodded and we put her in Lauren's single armchair. Dr. Bel went to the kitchen and gathered some wet paper towels, and Marly held her hands out like a child as Dr. Bel gently cleaned them off. The paper came away grey with soot and bits of skin.

"I found our girl here out on the corner," said Dr. Bel, smiling comfortingly up at Marly, who was trying not to wince. "She couldn't remember how to get in.

Dafne will be up in a minute—she's parking the car." For some reason the thought of that little thing driving a car struck me as funny, but I kept my face shut. "Well," Dr. Bel straightened up and looked March and me over. "That happened." She folded her arms. "What did we discuss about running off on your own?" I shrunk back against the couch. "You were supposed to be watching her," she said to Shanti, who looked embarrassed for the first time in our acquaintance.

"Sorry, Doctor Bel," she murmured. "I was sort of on a date..."

Dr. Bel turned to March. "And you—"

"Can I come out now?" Sasha stuck his head out of the bedroom. "Since all our principles have arrived and have started shouting at each other?" He didn't wait for an answer, but pulled a kitchen chair up to sit near Marly. He was looking at her pretty intensely.

"Sasha, this is my friend Marly. We've spoken about her. Mar, Sasha is from the, uh, Unseelie Court."

"I've heard of you," said Marly. "From the fox man. He liked to talk about you. He said you wanted to catch me and kill me."

He looked horrified. "Literally nothing could be further from the truth. In fact, it is my very great pleasure to finally meet you in person," he said. I gaped at him. His very great pleasure?

"Why?" she asked, which was a completely reasonable question.

He didn't exactly answer. "I know you've been through an ordeal recently. I admire your fortitude." Something was up. This was the nicest he'd been to anyone since he got here.

A knock at the door, and Dr. Bel went to let Dafne in. She was in the middle of telling Dr. Bel where she'd left the car when she stopped, stared for a second, and dropped to her knees. She pressed her forehead to the floor.

"You may rise," said Sasha.

"Please accept my apologies, my lord. I was not informed. I am without a gift, I'm not properly dressed—"

"What?" asked Dr. Bel.

"Bel," Dafne hissed, "why didn't you tell me the king himself would be here today?"

"The what now?" I said. "No, Dafne, this is Sasha."

"This is the king of the Unseelie Court, you idiot," she answered.

"I thought he looked familiar." March said.

"You recognized him? Why didn't you say anything?" I asked.

March held his hands up. "It was dark and he was wearing a helmet! And it was like four hundred years ago."

"Hey, what about the whole 'fae can't lie' thing?" Shanti asked.

"Yeah, what about that, *Sasha*?" I wanted to kill

him. "I gave you pizza! And you were lying the whole time!"

He looked at us, miffed. "I was not lying. I was acting. I know they're different, I saw it on the television." I think he was actually disappointed that he didn't get a round of applause on his masterful performance. I thought of the things I'd heard about the fae: heartless, debauched. Liars, after all.

Dr. Bel sighed. "I told you, they bend the truth to suit themselves." To Sasha she said, "You never did say, 'I am not the king,' did you?"

"Certainly not. Well, acting was certainly entertaining. I'll miss it. I understand why you humans are so addicted to it. But now —"

"Why are you here?" I asked. "Really? It wasn't about justice for Lauren, was it?"

"In a roundabout way. No, I'm here for this young lady." He extended a languid hand toward Marly. "I have cause to believe she is unique, rather like you, March. And in fact I have you to thank."

"What is he talking about?" Marly was shaking, and I quickly went to her side and put my arm around her. "What does that mean?"

"I think he means this." I pulled the wrinkled, blood-stained paper out of my pocket. "Can I let Doctor Bel look at this?" I asked. Marly nodded and I handed it over. She read it, frowning.

"She *is* unique," Dr. Bel finally said. "I'm not a

hematologist, but I took enough lab courses to see anomalies everywhere. I've never seen anything like this. But I'm not sure what it all adds up to."

"It adds up to something miraculous," Sasha said. "Anomaly is such an inelegant way of saying it. March, along with that unnamed vampire, conspired without knowing it to remake you. That page is the proof. You're like me now."

Marly cocked her head. "I'm an asshole?"

He smiled. Without looking away from Marly, he said, "Nymph, attend me." He pointed at his eyes. Dafne raced to the kitchen and got him a glass of water. He bent over and carefully removed the lens-creatures that made him appear almost human. When he looked back up, his eyes were completely black. The silver lights flickered quite near the surface.

Marly's jaw dropped. "But they're beautiful," she said. When he reached out to take off her sunglasses, she held still.

"And so are yours," he said. And they were.

"Whoa," said Shanti. "She's a..."

"I really should have known," said Dr. Bel.

Marly looked around at us with the all-black eyes of the fae. I could see golden lights darting in their endless depth. "I'm still me," she said. "Aren't I?" and started to sob. But to me it sounded like she was crying with relief.

27

"It began almost as soon as you and I had that stupid fight at the bar." Marly had quit crying and was back to eating—this time ice cream, right from the carton with a plastic spoon. "At first I thought I had some bullshit eye infection, maybe from the trip I took last year to Belize. Then I started burning myself on, like, everything."

"She is new-made," Sasha said, "and sensitive."

She glanced at him. Her strange new eyes made her look like a different person, spooky and gorgeous, but her mouth let me know she was still my friend. "Uh, yeah. Sensitive. So I went and got some oven mitts so I could do stuff like make coffee. But I didn't want anything but dessert." She sniffled. "And I hate dessert! I thought I was going to get fat and diabetes *and* die from the world's dumbest cancer."

"That's when you went to see Michael, wasn't it?" asked Dr. Bel.

Marly nodded. "He was really nice. I'm sorry about what happened to him."

"Why didn't you call me?" I asked. She stared at me for a long second. I looked away.

"Well, first I was mad at you, and then that...the man showed up. The fox man. I thought I was hallucinating, that it was part of whatever was wrong with me. He kept telling me I was bad, and it was my fault bad things were happening. He would hide the oven mitts, and wake me up all night. And he kept making the doors vanish." She dropped her head into her hands, and then yanked them away and shook her fingers with a hiss of pain. "The day you guys came looking for me, he made me call you." She covered her mouth. "Those things I said..."

"I know. It wasn't you."

"He said he'd find a way to hurt you worse, if I didn't hurt you then." She swallowed hard. "I hated you, for a little bit. And I blamed you. I had a lot to say, but those things, none of that was true. I'm so sorry."

"I already forgot it. When this is over you can tell me all the true stuff."

"Deal." I got a smile. Just a little one. "When we go to the spa. I think I can still touch hot rocks." She continued. "Anyway, he made me tell you to leave me alone. And then yesterday, I found my phone, and I texted you before he could stop me."

"I think he let you find it," I said. "But it doesn't matter. We took care of him." *Ask the king.* I looked up at Sasha. "Why did the *kitsune* go after Lauren?"

"I beg your pardon?"

"The *kitsune* said to ask the king who put Lauren in his path. So I'm asking."

He laughed. "You don't really intend to take the word of that creature? Your friend here just described him as a malodorous pest."

"I didn't say that," said Marly. "That he smelled."

"Well," Sasha said, "but, everyone knows that." He sounded nonchalant but I felt like maybe he was beginning to sweat.

"I didn't know that," said Dafne. "What do they smell like?"

"Cat piss," I said. Then I remembered. "Like I smelled outside Lauren's door the night I found her body." We all looked at each other. "Like I smell right now."

The door opened, and the *kitsune* lunged into the room. He didn't make it very far, as he was on a short leash. Tha yanked him back. He hissed, and I noticed that Sasha quickly moved in front of Marly. That was interesting. The fox looked up at Tha and whined.

Tha nodded at the animal. "You may, as long as you behave yourself."

"Dragon, I did not agree to this," said Sasha. He

looked pissed.

She shrugged. "You are not the king of my house. It's time for us to negotiate terms regarding the captive."

We watched as the fox became the man, and then I looked away because he was naked. Shanti ducked into the bathroom and came out with Lauren's pink bathrobe.

"Cover that nonsense up," she said, and tossed it to him.

He tied the sash; the robe barely came to his knees. "Are you proud of yourself," he asked me, "for ruining my life a second time?"

Marly grabbed my arm. "Keep him away from me." Her voice shook.

"You have something to say," Tha said to him, "so say it."

"I'll make this quick." The *kitsune* looked Marly over. She winced away from his gaze. "So the eyes are out of the bag, I see. Nice. Well, let's get to it. Your friend Sasha here hired me to find you. Everything that happened is on him."

We all turned and looked at Sasha, who was already trying to placate Marly.

"You know you can't trust him," he said. "You know what kind of a liar he is."

"I do," she said, "I know he's a liar. But how do *you* know?"

"I, uh, it is well known they are treacherous," he

said. Definitely sweating now.

"You may as well tell your girlfriend," the *kitsune* said.

"Not his girlfriend," said Marly. "But yeah, you may as well."

"Fine," Sasha pursed his lips. "I did hire this creature, since he lived next door, but only to gather information. I only wanted him to listen in on Lauren with the hope of finding out if you really existed."

"You *did* put her in his path," I said. *Kitsune*: 1, Sasha: nothing.

"Oh, you asked him about that! Well done. Right, anyway, I listened," said the fox, "with my one good ear." He glared at me. I shuddered. "I also went over there when she was out, read her notes, tried on her clothes..." he snickered and licked his teeth. "I learned all sorts of things...her stupid research project, a unicorn with waning powers, and a special girl, a very special girl who was so, so mad at her friend Ruby. That made two of us." He touched his scarred head. "Why do you think I took this job?"

"That's what I smelled the day we moved Lauren in," said Shanti. "I knew something was wrong."

He yawned. "The king here was happy to lap up whatever nonsense I told him. Poor Marly was sad and crazy, Ruby was sad and guilty, even the horse was having some feelings. Sad ones. And some others. Weren't you?" March looked away. "I let it drag on as long as I could, but the doctor nearly ruined everything."

"You told me the proof I needed was finally ready," said Sasha. "But you never delivered it."

"Well, that would have been too easy," said the fox. "I got it, though. Too bad the doc walked in when I was retrieving it. He really shouldn't have kept important papers at his house. Oh well, lesson learned."

"I should kill you for that myself," said Dr. Bel. Dafne took her hand.

"The doctor texted Lauren, and then she texted you, Rubes." He looked mournfully at the ceiling. "If only you were a better friend, you might have bothered to read her text and maybe even save her life. But sure, your little job is so much more important."

Hearing him say it out loud made it feel true, even though I knew it wasn't. I should have let the dragon burn him.

"You killed them both?" Dr. Bel looked repulsed. "You took two lives in one night?"

The fox shrugged. He actually looked bored. "The little bitch wouldn't hand over her phone." He smiled. "It was an accident."

"It was an iron bar through our sister's chest." Sasha looked like he wanted to dismantle the *kitsune* on the spot. I was surprised to see Marly put a restraining hand on his arm.

"Why did you need her phone?" she asked. "And where is it now?"

"It had that text from ol' Doc Kennedy on it. And it had Marly's number, too. That would have been cheating. And I didn't have time to dick around erasing everything, so by now its probably at the bottom of a landfill someplace. Anyway, once I got our Lauren situation sorted, I figured it was time to bounce. Poor crazy Marly got herself a new roommate." Marly covered her eyes with her hands, and he grinned. "After what these two did to me last year, I've been waiting for the opportunity to return the favor. That's why I moved into this disgusting city, I was no longer able to stand the rigors of the forest. Then, when Marly started, um, *anomalyzing* I figured it would be the perfect way to get the job done. And when Lauren moved in next door, I made sure the king knew I was open for business."

"You would use this lady as bait?" Sasha looked livid. "You knew where she was all along?"

"Seriously, let's not forget the king was still lying to all of you the entire time," said the *kitsune*. "If you're all looking for someone to blame. After all, I was just his tool. The Courts will love hearing about this." He cocked his head. "Maybe 'love' is the wrong word."

"You seem awfully eager to tell us what happened," I said.

He grinned. "Now none of you can say you don't know the king's secrets, in case he gets any funny ideas. And anyway, it's not done happening, is it?" Then he looked at Sasha. "You're going to let me go, right?"

"What? Why would I do that?"

"Well," said the fox, "Here's where it gets interesting. Let's say you do what you've got in mind—take me back as your captive. You'll have to return poor Lauren's body to the Seelie Court, yes? So, I'm just guessing, but I bet they'll want to know what happened to her. They'll demand you produce your captive. And when I get in front of them, I'll tell them what happened. I'll tell them she killed their fae." And he pointed at Marly. "Not the kind of attention you're looking for, is—*yip*!"

Sasha was on him before we could even blink. I don't know where he'd been hiding it, but he had his long knife at the fox's throat. "Say her name. Give me a reason."

The fox looked down at the knife under his chin, but didn't miss a beat.

"Or let's say you give in to your baser impulses right now and go back alone. Can't tell the Seelie Court I acted alone, that's a big fat lie. And even though you want to, I don't think you'll kill me in front of all of you—my witnesses. Of course, you could give me to the dragon, but that would be a display if weakness, wouldn't it?" Without turning his head, he looked at Marly. "They hate that. Thank me later."

"What does that mean?" Marly asked.

The fox man showed her his yellow teeth but didn't answer. He looked back up at Sasha. "Would you mind?" Sasha took a step back, and when he opened his hand, the knife had vanished. The fox wiped the bead of blood off his neck and licked his finger, then nodded approvingly. I tried not to gag. "Or hey, maybe you bring me back and accuse me, and they believe you. Darn it, we're back to you hiring me and then keeping Lauren's death a secret. And the death of that human doctor. That was on your watch too. Tell me, when was there last a war between the Courts? But, if you let me go, you can tell the Seelie Court you delivered the king's justice and you'll never hear from me again."

Done with his speech, he grinned at Sasha, who looked down his nose dispassionately. "I relinquish rights to the captive. Dragon, he is yours."

Tha looked surprised for a split second. "I accept."

"You're giving me away?" The fox was incredulous. "To *her*? After what I just said? No! No. Um. It won't be like you think. The dragon and I, we'll have a lot to talk about. Does she know your secrets? All of them? I'll make sure she does."

"On one condition," Sasha added. "Keep him on four paws."

"We will have a conversation about secrets, Lord King, but that can wait for another day." She snapped her fingers and the man turned back into the one-eared fox. He stepped daintily out of the robe. "If we are done here," Tha said, slapping the end of leash against her palm, "Its time for you to wrap this up. All of you, time to leave my house." To Marly she said, "Good luck, child," in a much kinder voice. Then she looked down at the fox. "Come along. You need a flea bath."

The fox growled but kept his head down. He followed Tha out of the apartment, and the zoo smell slowly faded away.

"Well," said Dr. Bel. "That was convenient. I think it's time you explained yourself, 'Lord King.'"

Sasha sighed. "Very well." He looked at Marly with an expression that might have been affection. "I did all of this for you."

28

Sasha began his apology by telling us how lucky we were to be in the same room with him.

"I don't expect any of you to understand how rare this is, that I should explain myself." We all looked at him with expressions ranging from wide-eyed curiosity—that would be Dafne, to flat out suspicion from March. "Just be aware this is an honor. You should be honored."

I stuck my hand up. "Who's feeling honored? I sure am."

He began to give me his typical glare, then remembered he was trying to make friends. "If I may continue? Allow me to begin at my court, the Fair Home, the Seat of Wonder—"

"It's nice," said Dafne. "I've been." Ha, the little name dropper.

"Yes," Sasha agreed. "Nice. But we of the Unseelie Court are facing a threat, something none of us could have predicted. Dark and troubling times have come. The seed of our men no longer flowers in the grottos of our women."

Marly was looking my way, and despite her fancy new eyes, we made eye contact and both had to struggle to keep from cracking up. Grottos? What the hell?

Sasha folded his arms. "Is this amusing in some way?"

Shanti spoke up. "A thousand pardons, Lord King. It's a rather unusual turn of phrase. We live in a more clinical world. It's not in the least funny." She was shooting orange-hued daggers at me and Marly, and we managed to settle down.

"Perhaps the impending extinction of my people is a joke?" he asked.

"Is that what that meant?" I asked. Was he talking about children? Or lack of children? I'd never heard of a uterus referred to as a grotto before but I guess it made sense. Okay, that was not funny. Sorry, Sasha.

He appeared to have abandoned his friendship tour and gave us all a round of glares. "I heard, as we of the Courts sometimes do, of interesting events in the mortal realm last year. The unicorn. The woman who saved him. And of you, Marly. I had to find out if the rumors were true before the Seelie Court got their hands on you. They have their own troubles, but they are less refined in their constitutions and more able to commingle with the mortal world. Lauren herself wrote of such a thing. And the fox made himself available. He was in the story, too."

"You knew what he was about and you hired him anyway?" I think the glare I gave him back was fae-worthy.

"I knew he was familiar with the players and already on the scene. He was living next to Lauren."

"And that didn't strike you as dangerous?" Dr. Bel asked.

"It didn't strike me as anything, because I was only concerned about finding Marly. Had I known he would harass her, I would have made different decisions." He turned to her. "I would have never let him speak your name, much less torment you as he did."

"What did he say about me?" she asked.

"He was evasive. He said you were...He said you seemed troubled, and thought there was some truth to what I'd heard."

I wondered what he'd really said about her.

"Which was what?" Marly was watching Sasha, but with her new eyes, I couldn't tell what she was thinking.

"Rumors of something new," he told her. "Something miraculous. A child of the eternal death of the vampire and the endless life of the unicorn. A fae made not by birth, but by re-birth. Someone strong. I would be no leader of my people if I didn't investigate."

"But things began to go wrong, didn't they?" Dr. Bel said.

Sasha nodded, seemingly annoyed by Dr. Bel being a step ahead of his story. "The fox began to miss his audiences with me. He became more and more secretive. He refused to say what he'd found out about you. He promised but did not deliver results on paper, which seemed outlandish to me at the time, but appears to be an actual thing. He swore he didn't know where you could be found. And then he vanished completely."

"And you came looking for him." March spoke for the first time. "What did you find?"

"I found his home empty, except for his scent, which I followed it into the hallway and to the dwelling next door. And there I found the body of our sister Lauren, dead on the floor. I had to decide what to do, and quickly. The fox told me everyone in the story was stupid and malicious. I considered that I might be completely without allies in my search. The fox left the note—from you, Bel, with the name of a doctor on it, and numbers. It was my only clue. Then you showed up, Ruby. I may have reacted poorly."

"No wonder you were so rude." My fingers went to my throat. I couldn't help but remember the night we met, and the feel of that cold black metal glove around my neck. He watched me doing it and must have been thinking the same thing.

"I quickly realized you were not stupid. I left for

home to try and decide what to do next, when I learned another of the ladies at court had her blossom wither and die." Obviously, none of us were laughing any more. "She was one of the youngest and, we hoped, most likely to bear fruit. I had no choice. I had to conceal Lauren's death and trust you—the group of you—to lead me to Marly."

"But what about me?" Marly asked. "I'm like you—like the fae. I get that. But what makes me so important?"

Sasha knelt next to her chair. "I was hoping to have this conversation more privately, but here we are. As I said, I came here for you; a remarkable woman, no longer quite human, who carries the fae in her blood. Marly, my people are an old, old race. I will be blunt—we are dying out. You are young, from a young race. You are fae enough to be one of us, and human enough to carry forward our line."

"I know you aren't saying what I think you're saying." Her eyes were wide and expressionless but her lips curled in distaste.

"It's exactly what I'm saying. You could save us all, Marly. I am inviting you to come back to the Unseelie Court and be my queen."

She opened and closed her mouth once or twice. Finally, she said, "Why didn't you just, like, kidnap me or something?"

He laughed. "We are not a pack of savages! I was going to kidnap her." He pointed at me. "And wait for you to come and retrieve your friend." We gaped at each other, and then looked back at him. "That's how we would have handled it at my court. In retrospect it might not have been a viable plan. At any rate, I was hoping to spend time with you before discussing this, but I see your progression has gone far beyond what I expected. You know it yourself, you can't stay here. You need help. My help." He took her hand and turned it palm up. It was blistered. She'd been touching iron.

"And that poor girl's body?" Dr. Bel came and stood behind Marly.

"It will be returned to her people as soon as possible."

"That is not an answer." I was glad to see Dr. Bel stepping up—for Marly and for Lauren. I wondered who would stand up for the doctor, and how.

"I said I was taking her home. I did. To my home, where she rests right now."

"He hid the body," said March. "Didn't you?"

Sasha looked like he wanted to take March's head off, and I remembered the Field of Significant Contact. They had worked together for a bit, but they were not allies. "She will be reunited with her people as soon as I return to my court. I may have made...mistakes, but I hope you'll believe I never wanted that creature to harm anyone. Certainly not you, Marly. He was, as you mortals say, off the reservation."

"So, that's kind of racist," said Marly. She turned to

us. “Do we believe him?”

Sasha spread his hands. “I was taken advantage of just as much as the rest of you.”

“Please,” I said, “please say that you’re the real victim here.”

“The fox took this job as a pretext to attack you and March. Fortunately, his anger towards you made him sloppy. You prevailed.” He stood. “When the Seelie Court asks what happened to Lauren, I’ll tell them my agent turned against me, but that the king’s justice has been delivered. Because it has. And now that we’ve got everything settled, Marly, please consider accompanying me to the Fair Seat, where we live in grace and peace. I’d be honored to show you my home, which I hope you’ll one day come to think of as your home.”

Marly took a deep breath. “I’ll go with you—on a couple of conditions. One—I get to leave whenever I want, no questions asked, no escort, no one following me back here.”

“This is unwise and you will almost certainly change your mind, but for now, done.”

“Two. Leave my friends out of this. Whatever happens between you and me, they don’t get involved.”

Dr. Bel spoke up. “She means to include her family, her friends, students current and former, and her general acquaintances. She further demands there’ll be no hostages taken, no revenge by incantation or otherwise, and no *vendetta aux sortilege*."

"And absolutely no assassination," Shanti added.

Sasha gave a disdainful shrug. I bet he had each and every one of those things lined up and ready to go. "As you say. Thank you for assisting my queen."

"I'm not your queen yet, pal." Marly was still pale and shook, but she was getting her feet under her. "Right. Um. Three. I will tell you when it's time to talk about the bloodlines and all that stuff. No pressure, or I'll bail."

"Done."

Marly turned and took my hand as best she could. "I know you think this is a bad idea—"

I nodded. "Cause it is." Even if Sasha hadn't physically murdered anyone, he was still a stone liar, and the one thing everyone knew about his people was that they couldn't lie. What else were we wrong about? I was tempted to offer to go with her myself. Maybe there was a way.

Marly continued. "But I can't stay here. I have to learn how to be this...whatever I am. It's not only my body that's different. I'm different in my head. I have to figure myself out. Do you understand?"

"I want to say no, but I get it. Promise me if things get weird, you call me. Okay? I'll come and get you. Swear."

She smiled for real, the first one I'd seen since we fought. "I know you will. I love you, dope. Maybe the Unseelie Court gets cell service?" She looked at Sasha, who shook his head. "Well, then I'll send a letter. I promise. Swear it. And soon. And if this guy tries anything, you, me, and Shanti will take him down. Deal?"

"Deal." Shanti's eyes had an orange bloom to them. I think she was looking forward to that part.

Marly got to her feet. "March, take care of my girl. Doctor Bel, short lady, thanks for coming to help me." She took a step towards Sasha, and vanished.

29

"Your realm is not inaccessible," Dr. Bel said to the fucking king of the Unseelie Court. "I'll be expecting updates on how Marly is progressing. And don't think the question of who is responsible for those deaths has been answered to my satisfaction. A human life was also taken, and some of us chose to live here among them."

He was the only person I'd ever seen not be intimidated or even slightly impressed with Dr. Bel when she gets her goddess thing going. But then, he was also the only king I'd ever met. "You heard the *kitsune*. Was that not a confession? Was it not his hand who held the iron bar?" He held up his own hand, now gloveless. "It wasn't mine. And as far as Marly, when there is something to say, I'll make sure she says it." I think he was eager to leave, to go home, toss his gloves, and show off his queen-to-be.

"I think you guys can take off," I said to the three women. "I'd like to have a chat with the king before he heads out. You do have a few minutes, don't you? *Sasha*?"

He said he did. Then he turned to Shanti. "Oh, and may I count on you to join me at my court for a hunt sometime in the near future?"

"Um, I don't kn—"

I cut her off. "She'd be delighted." I made owl eyes at her. This was the way in. "Won't you?"

It only took her a second. "Why, yes. I believe I'd enjoy a hunt at your court."

Sasha laughed. "Look at this—a scheme! And me here to witness it, damp and newly hatched. I do look forward to seeing how it plays out."

Bel gave him a curt nod, and Dafne hit the floor again. Bel pulled her up by the collar. "We don't kneel, you and I." To me she said, "You call me this week, okay? Like, tomorrow."

I agreed that would be a good idea. Finally it was just the three of us; me, March, and Sasha.

"Well," said Sasha, "I do owe you both—"

"You lying sack of shit," I said. "Acting like this was so hard. Like you didn't know who killed Lauren the whole goddamn time. I trusted you."

"He can't help his nature," March said. "Any more than the *kitsune* can."

Sasha twisted his lips in something like a smile. "Thank you for being so understanding."

"That's not what I meant," March countered. "You figured out a way to lie—by pretending it was a game. You put Ruby in danger. You think I'm understanding? Hardly."

"Interesting how you think I'm the one who put her in danger. But I'll try and explain myself once again. You are free to ignore me and feel betrayed, or you can try and see this from my perspective. My people are dying. Not soon, but soon enough, we will cease to exist. Marly won't survive here by herself. Do I wring my hands and hope for the best? Or do I act—in my own best interest, and in hers? What would you have done?"

"You still should have told me," I said.

He sighed. "I will arrange for a *fête* in Lauren's honor at my own court. You won't understand how rare and important this will be, but I assure you she will not be forgotten. Believe it or not, I'm sorry you were misled, Ruby. You're a good friend to Marly and a good representative of your own people. To show my appreciation for your service, I'm going to give you a gift. It's actually for both of you, since you both helped me bring Marly home."

"What sort of gift?" March had his hairs up. He went into this not trusting Sasha, and he was right all along. He put a protective hand on my shoulder. "His gifts come at a price." He paused. "That's not actually what a gift is, though, is it?"

"Sure not," I said. "But let's see what he's got in mind."

Sasha folded his arms. "Would you like to cure your time problem? Because I know how to do it."

We looked at each other. "What? How?" I asked.

"You're the key, Ruby. I think you already knew that." He turned to March. "She is the rock in your river, haven't you said that?"

"She is my shiny stone," he agreed. "I keep seeing her, but it's hard to say when." He leaned towards me, suddenly confused. He'd done magic. The charm had been broken. "This is now, right?"

"You got it," I said. "Hang in there. So, what is it about me? Why does he keep slipping?"

"I keep coming back to her, she is my fixed point." March said.

"Let's continue to go with our time as a river analogy. What happens when you put a rock in a river?"

March thought for a moment. "It gives you something to stand on. Or a way to cross the water."

"But," Sasha said, "you're not trying to cross. Or to stand still. You wish to move forward with time, and flow."

"Oh," I said. "Oh, no." I took March's hands in my own. "When you put a rock in the river, it screws with the current. It makes eddies and...and whirlpools. Am I right?" Sasha nodded. "I'm not your fixed point. I'm the reason your river isn't flowing."

"Because of this mortal girl, you did something none of your kind can claim—you made a sacrifice. Baba Yaga held her out for trade. You gave your own life willingly and became something new. Not as marvelous as my Marly, but new and interesting nonetheless. You experience time. I don't believe any of your people can say the same. You have memory and anger and regret and, if I'm not mistaken, love. But you also cannot fix yourself in time. You can't tell the difference between memory and actuality. Why? Ruby is standing between you and time in its normal course."

"My shiny stone," March said softly.

"But what can we do about it?" I asked. "I don't want to be the reason he keeps slipping."

"There's a couple of things. I don't think you'll care for the most obvious one, which is for me to end your life and remove you from the river."

"Um, no thank you," I said. March moved in front of me.

"Don't worry, unicorn, I won't touch her. The other, less fatal option is for me to remove her from your time stream by removing her memories of you. You will look for your fixed point, but she won't be there. To her, you won't ever have happened. To you, she will merely be a shimmer on the water—to be recalled, but never relived. I can't remove your memories—being what you are, you have far too many." He smiled thinly. "As I think you are coming to realize."

I took a step towards him. "I don't believe you. I think you're just trying to get back at March for getting away from you all those years ago."

Sasha raised his brow. "You're calling me a liar. How remarkable. Well. Perhaps you'd prefer to hear it from Lauren. You did trust Lauren, no?" He picked the stack of paper back up off the table. "I continued to study her notes. A shame you and I didn't get this far, it was enlightening." He shuffled through the fragile sheets. "Ah. This is from just last week.

I fear my investigation is harder on Ruby than I'd anticipated. Every time we talk about the unicorn I can see the sadness she carries. From my studies of both species I know she's unlikely to 'get over him' as humans often do when besotted with each other. His kind cannot so easily be forgotten. I wonder if she'd have been better off if their paths had never crossed. She can't stop asking herself if what she feels for him is real, and worse, she has to wonder if he felt anything for her at all. Certainly the unicorn—wherever he is—is experiencing the results of living in a mortal shell, much as our Aello once did. Of course in his case if Ruby hadn't appeared when she did, he would not have survived, so even though he may be experiencing time displacement, from his perspective it's better than the alternative. The question remains as to how much time he has left, and where he will choose to spend that time—and with whom." Sasha looked up at me. "There are many other references to," he looked back down, ruffling through the pages, "your depression and anxiety. She thought you were foolish to abandon your therapy."

My face burned. Had I been that obvious? "What if we don't do anything?"

Sasha looked at March. "He knows. He knows the story of Aello."

"I will come unstuck," said March. He sounded miserable. "I will wander my own mind and never know what's real."

"In a way, I'm giving you two gifts," Sasha said brightly. "One for each of you. Unicorn, you get your mind back, and you'll be free to do whatever it is your kind call having a life, unencumbered by all this human nonsense."

March looked at him warily. "I'll be as I was before?"

"Before your mortal week last year? I think not. It's a gift, not a miracle. You'll keep your newfound emotions. You'll still feel the passage of time. But you won't be lost in it." He looked impatiently at the two of us. "Isn't this what you want?"

March looked at me. "It's what I wanted once. But now..."

"And you, Ruby. You'll never have to spend another second wondering if he'll appear, or what you mean to him. You'll also be free."

I wiped my eyes with my sleeve. "And this is your

idea of a gift? You're a monster."

Sasha looked at me thoughtfully and nodded. "I am the worst. I told you that when we met. That, at least, was no act."

"What do you want me to say? You told the truth one time, hooray. You thoroughly suck, Sasha."

He looked at me, amused. "I am going to miss our little exchanges. No one at my court speaks to me the way you do. I have to admit I enjoy it. It's bracing."

"Well, prepare to be full-time braced because Marly tells the truth too. And the truth is this is no gift."

"Isn't it? I am saving him from losing his mind, and saving you from..." he looked down his nose, "him. You'll be far better off without this creature in your life."

And the thing is, I think he meant it. "But what about everyone else? They'll try and remind me, won't they?"

He nodded. "And it'll make you feel slightly ill, and you won't really listen to their questions. You humans are good at that, ignoring the uncomfortable. Your mind will fill in the blanks and come up with a new story. Eventually, they'll stop asking. Now, I'm going to go gather my things, so do what you need to do. I'll be back a few minutes." He went to the bedroom, I guess to pack his bag of dicks.

March held me tight. I clung to him, trying to burn the memory of his shape into my mind. I couldn't believe I'd forget him. Since the day we met I'd done nothing but picture his face. He said, "What if he's lying? What if it's not worth it?"

"I think...I think it's not a trick. But if it is, find Bel. She made him swear he wouldn't try anything against us. And if this works, if you're saved, then it was worth it."

"I haven't even gotten to love you yet," he said. "That's why I came back here, and I didn't even know what it was called. This is the first time I ever wanted to stay. I know you won't remember, but I will. Don't cry. I'll never forget you. Never." And he kissed me for the last time, and it was as sweet as the first.

Sasha came back out with his black leather duffel bag. "It's time," he said.

"I love you," I said.

"I'll find a way," March whispered. "I'll fix this. I'll come back for you." And then—

30

"**...and then Marly agreed to** go with him," I told James. "I mean, obviously I don't trust ol' King Sasha as far as I can throw him, but I have to admit, I think it's for the best."

"He is a man of his word. Well, not exactly a man," James replied. "And only words he chooses himself. If he said he will help your friend, I think he will. He went to a great deal of trouble to secure her."

"Yeah, agreed. His whole 'save my people' thing kind of falls apart without her cooperation." I snickered. "Mother of her people. Well, we'll see." I yawned. "At least she'll get a chance to heal and figure out what she can and can't touch. Get used to being an Unseelie fae." I shook my head. "I knew something was weird when she got bitten. I mean, I didn't believe it was a spider bite, even a big-ass tropical spider wouldn't do that. I'm just so glad they were able to bring her back."

"They?"

"Yeah, the doctors. At the resort in Belize. Miracle workers, I swear. And we never would have known. They said something...I don't know exactly...something activated in her blood after that. And there you go. Boom. Fae. And Sasha did say she could come back anytime she wanted. I know my girl, she'll hold him to it." I'd miss her like crazy, but if being in that strange place could make her whole, she could have all the time she needed. I also looked forward to hearing how she was going to get Mr. Sasha-I-Was-Just-Acting to fall in line. And there was my plan—okay, it wasn't quite a plan yet—to go with Shanti for a visit to the Unseelie Court.

"Anything else happen?" he asked. "At all? That you remember?"

I snorted. "Isn't that enough? No, that's plenty for one night. Oh, I have to let Ray and Sheena know. Their favorite teacher might be the next Queen of the Fairies, I bet they'll dig that." I yawned again, and winced when I brushed my bandaged leg against the car door. It was kind of funny how small the bruise on my knee was, considering how hard the *kitsune* hit me. I thought for sure I would have needed stitches, but it didn't look that bad. Oh well, I guess I just got lucky. "Maybe things can start to get back to normal around here. I'm having lunch with Shanti tomorrow. We've got to set up our spa date, and she'll want to know if I ever told—"

"If you told...?"

" If I ever told..." I stopped, and fought back a sudden wave of nausea. Just as quickly, it faded away. "How weird. I don't know. I know I was...well, I'm sure it isn't important. She can remind me."

We pulled to a stop in front of my house. James took his king's medal off its spot hanging from the rearview, and let it dangle on its silk cord between his fingers. As it twirled I could see the tree/cloud/dragon appear and vanish. "I am tasked to give you this."

This looked like a gift to me. "Will this put me in your debt, now? Or the king's? I wanted to put some space between myself and Sasha. Like, a whole planet's worth.

He gave me a serious look. "It is not a gift. And if you refuse it, then I will have failed. However, if you take it, I'm finished. You're my last fare. Ever."

"You'll be free of your debt, you mean?" He nodded. Another impossible choice. Thanks, Sasha. Of course I took the silver disk. It was warm on my palm, and the dome light gave it a sort of orange glow. I wondered what it was for. I would certainly find out. "Well, go ahead and be free. Are you staying in town?"

He laughed. "I don't mean to imply this city is an overcrowded dump, so let's just say I prefer warmer weather. I'm going south, I'm going home."

"Good luck, then, and thank you. For everything."

I got out and he drove off, blinking his lights in a

farewell. I waved, and then I was alone.

Inside, I tossed the medallion on my dresser, and threw my backpack in the corner. Out of the corner of my eye I caught a flash of something shiny that fell out and bounced under the bed. I reached down and retrieved it. Small, black and plastic. A phone. One of those cheap burner phones you buy at the corner store. I wondered how it got into my bag and who it belonged to, and powered it up.

"Huh," I said to the room, "that's funny." There was only one number programmed into it—mine. No call log, though. I sat on the edge of the bed and scrolled around. It looked like there were a couple of texts, but they disappeared almost before I could make them out. All I could see were a couple of letters—M-a-r—and they were gone. The little screen went blank.

"Mar...Marly?" Who else could it have been? The way the texts dissolved made me think the phone had a bad chip—these things weren't very well made—and it was time to toss it. But after I threw it in my trashcan, I changed my mind and fished it out. I pulled out the drawer in my nightstand and pushed the hand cream and pens and whatnot to the side, and set it in the back. I mean, the owner might come back looking for it one day.

You never know, right?

31

March

I **didn't see Sasha do anything** that might be called magic—unlike his trick with the hidden blade. He didn't use his hands or recite a spell, he just set his shiny black duffel on the kitchen table. But he must have done something, because by the time he turned back to us, Ruby had begun to sag in my arms.

"Wow, sorry," she said, quickly pulling away from me. "Thought I was going to pass out for a sec. I guess I'm dehydrated or something." Her eyes never met mine, and she put her hands on her hips to confront Sasha. "You'll be hearing from me, champ." Then her expression softened. "Take care of Marly. That's your one job."

"In that we are in agreement," he answered.

She left without a backward glance. I wanted to reach out to her, call her name, demand she come back, but I knew she wouldn't respond, and I didn't wish to appear weak in front of the king. Whatever Sasha had done to her, it worked. It remained to be seen if he'd effected a change in me as well.

"You ought to be going as well," said Sasha. "Enjoy your new, unencumbered life."

"Does anyone leave your presence without a threat?" I asked. I wasn't used to anger. I understood combat, but this was different. This was personal. Unlike a challenge accepted, this made my heart ache and my head pound. I didn't want to conquer Sasha on the field of battle, I wanted to hurt him, here and now.

He didn't seem to notice. "You're welcome, I'm sure. No need to worry about Ruby. Her friends will watch out for her." He walked to the door and opened it. Outside was everything that came after. Outside was one more thing I had to do. The door closed behind me.

I paused and leaned against the wall in the empty hallway, and I went looking. First, a rush of nearly ecstatic relief as I felt myself sink into the book of my life—instead of panic and dislocation, I was in control.

Here are the young couple on the beach, there are my long years of wandering alone in the forest. I smile at Bel, who peers up at me through the moonlit veil of her hair, I pass a black bull standing watch in a snow-covered field, here's a jay scolding me from a springtime branch, and now I hear music drifting up from a group of laughing humans—all at once, and all as alive as if I were there with them right now. Right now is right now, though, and I find that at last I can tell the difference.

The only thing missing was Ruby.

I reached for a memory to join her in, and the image shattered like I'd thrust my hand into water. She was there, but not there. I felt as if we'd barely begun to put our feet on a path meant to be traveled together, that together we would have explored this craving, this desire, the love I had for her, for that's what it was called. Instead I found myself alone on that strange road, and for the first time in my life, alone was not a place I wanted to be. My anger at Sasha began to fade. I assumed my love for Ruby would also fade. But I could go and visit my last encounter with Sasha, and the anger would be waiting for me, fresh and hot. Not so with Ruby. One day, whether it be in one year or one thousand, she'd be gone, and I'd be what I've always been. Alone.

Sasha's 'gift' to me.

"This isn't the end," I told Ruby and myself, and I headed towards my last stop before I went home to my woods. I walked past buildings and dogs and people, and watched as the cars flew past me. I smiled to think of how Ruby wasn't afraid of them at all, and I stopped walking as the pain which rode alongside memory stabbed my heart. Only memory. I breathed the dirty bus air and the clean garden air and the broken bags of garbage air of the city, and I wondered if I'd miss it, if I'd choose to relive those moments, even if Ruby wasn't there as anything other than a ghost.

I didn't think I would.

I arrived at my destination. A three-story building of tan brick with a fenced off yard and people standing around talking. The yard was little more than a square of packed dirt with some toys scattered here and there, but there were flowers growing in the windowsills and music coming from somewhere inside. I noticed the toys—for climbing and throwing and imagining worlds beyond the fence—were neglected and dusty. The people were sad. I saw tears on some faces, and for a moment I wondered if I was too late. They turned to look at me curiously; I was not from around there. Then I saw a woman I recognized, and I thought she knew me too. From inside the open sliding door in the first-floor apartment, I could hear the little girl; coughing and coughing. Her mother ran inside and carried the child out in her arms. One of her neighbors opened the gate and I went to meet them. The child was now too ill to walk, but her thin face lit up when she saw me.

I looked at her mother, at the people in the yard. I looked at my human hands one last time. "Tápate los ojos," I told them. "Cover your eyes."

Epilogue

Claims of miraculous cure greet police investigating reports of explosion

By Ann Berenbaum, staff writer

Police called to a reported explosion in the 600 block of Lamont Street North West Tuesday found instead a celebration among neighbors who told officers they had just witnessed a miracle.

According to their report, a series of 911 calls had reported an apparent transformer explosion following a blinding flash of light shortly after 3 p.m.

Instead, they found the family of 10, who told police that they had gathered to console the parents of a three-year-old girl diagnosed recently with a terminal illness.

'This morning, we thought it might be her last," the child's uncle, translating for the parents who seeking a cure for their daughter, recently arrived from El

Salvador, told police. "She was so pale, and thin. She could only cough."

"Milagro," the child's mother told police as her daughter raced, laughing and shouting around the home's front yard, according to their report. "Un milagro absoluto."

"El unicornio!" the child said, who police described as a healthy, active three-year-old.

The child's uncle confirmed to police that the family members believed a visiting unicorn had caused the commotion that had led neighbors to report an explosion, and had also cured the child of her illness.

Seeing no evidence of a unicorn, or of the reported explosion, police issued a warning to family and neighbors that making a false police report is a crime.

Ruby and March will be back! You can find out more about this series and the work of Kim Alexander by signing up for her newsletter.

Acknowledgements:

First, thank you to everyone who loved my cast of weirdos in Pure and have been cheerleading this series.
(Looking at you, Barbara!)
A river of thank you's to Dyon, as always.
Matthew the djinn and Michael, who finally made it into a book—sorry about the murder!
Dan Bloom, who made the audiobook of Pure possible.
Carly Hayward, the editing angel (and sometimes devil) on my shoulder.
Cait Reynolds, who proofed this thing into submission. (And who will take my em-dashes from my cold, dead hand.)
Aurelia Fray of Pretty AF Designs for another delicious cover.
Gladys Gonzales Atwell, publicist to the stars.
My town of D.C. City of Trees and Xenos, which is home to so much more than the government. Come to Adams Morgan and have a Jumbo Slice, then go to the National Zoo and visit the sea lions!

Also by Kim Alexander

New World Magic:

Pure

The Demon Door:

The Sand Prince

The Heron Prince

The Glass Girl

About the author:

Kim Alexander grew up in the wilds of Long Island, NY and slowly drifted south until she reached Key West. After spending ten rum-soaked years as a DJ in the Keys, she moved to Washington DC, where she lives with two cats, an angry fish, and her extremely patient husband.

Please visit her at kimalexanderonline.com

Made in the USA
Lexington, KY
28 September 2019